DANIEL ERIC FINKEL

Mr. Taffle's PANTS OF INSANITY

First Edition

ISBN   979-8-9868178-0-4 (ebook)
ISBN   979-8-9868178-1-1 (paperback)
ISBN   979-8-9868178-2-8 (hardback)

This is a work of fiction. All of the characters, organizations, and events portrayed in this novel are either the products of the author's imagination or are used fictitously. Any correlations to real life are purely coincidental.

Cover design by Patricia Moffett.
Author photo by Jesse Branum at Third Eye Visuals
Interior Design by FormattedBooks

DEDICATION

I dedicate this book to the memory of my mother Ruth Ann "Honey" Miller Finkel. She had the biggest heart I've ever known and I miss her every day.

Contents

Oh you brave reader! I see that you're about to slip on the Pants of Insanity and embark on one wild and weird ride. If you're nervous (as you should be) and feel like you need to try on the pants first, I recommend listening to the music EP that is based on the novel. It's available on all streaming platforms. Also, you can get exclusive access, insights, deals, discounts for all things Daniel Eric Finkel at danielericfinkel.com/SignUp.

CHAPTER ONE

Birth, Death, Birth

"That was the 365th best sunrise of the year," joked stereotypical Farmer Ted 1 to stereotypical Farmer Ted 2, as they watched a magnificent fake sun blast its florescent light across a field of cows, each of which had two basketball-sized udders. A chorus of rooster caws blasted over loudspeakers, and the smell of slightly-off sausage and cheddar grits piped through the vents; it always smelled the same. Farmer Ted 1's sunrise joke was always delivered in a deadpan style, which Old Man "Mongoose" McGeester had once called "genius." As a result, Farmer Ted 1 repeated the joke every morning, and Farmer Ted 2 never stopped pretending to laugh—which is what is required when you've been someone's number two for nearly your entire life.

Now, while it was true that Farmer Ted 1 had never farmed a day in his life, he was dedicated to waking up at the crack of dawn to bark orders at Farmer Ted 2. And this was the day it all became worth it: One of the two-udder cows was going to give birth. She had not been impregnated; thus, Farmer Ted 1 had named this pregnant cow Mary. Now, as Farmer Ted 1 yanked the gooey calf out, he was about to proclaim that this immaculately conceived calf be named Jeeees... But then, he stopped mid-sentence to spit out his wad of chewing tobacco (which landed only a centimeter from Farmer Ted 2's left eyeball). He continued, "Geez, why don't I call her My Best Friend." Farmer Ted 2 thought this name could be very misleading since he was Farmer Ted 1's best friend. However, just as some of the chew spit dripped off his left eyelash, he remembered that his opinion meant "less than a cow paddy on a stick," as Farmer Ted 1 reminded him daily.

And then the most amazing thing since the construction of the Underground Farm of the Two-Udder Cows happened: My Best Friend did a front flip-and-a-half and stuck the landing in a perfect handstand.

"Did you see that?" squealed Farmer Ted 1.

Farmer Ted 2 had been watching his own cremation in a restaurant-sized wood-fire pizza oven play out in his head and hadn't seen the flip-and-a-half. Even so, he promptly responded, "Yep."

❧ NINE MONTHS LATER ☙

Farmer Ted 1 stared intensely at My Best Friend as she grazed next to a line of six other cows while taking a large dump. My Best Friend quickly turned around and made direct eye contact with Farmer Ted 1. He immediately looked away, but My Best Friend clearly busted him watching her.

My Best Friend then trotted away toward the back wall (painted as a second-rate mural of the underground farm's fake horizon). She pressed herself against the wall, pushed off with her hind legs, and sprinted like a fat cheetah straight into the line of cows. The cows toppled over like cow dominoes.

"DID YOU SEE THAT?!" Farmer Ted 1 squealed.

"Yep," replied Farmer Ted 2, even though he had once again been daydreaming—this time about being reincarnated as a giant stingray.

⋘ ONE YEAR LATER ⋙

"Oh, what amazing times we had watching My Best Friend grow up, perform gymnastics, and play demented practical jokes," reflected Farmer Ted 1. He squeezed Farmer Ted 2's limp, clammy right hand for 22 seconds. Old Man "Mongoose" McGeester had advised Farmer Ted 1 that showing affection would be a major action step in his quest to give a crap about anyone. But Farmer Ted 1 really did feel something for My Best Friend. He secretly wished he lived in a world where she wouldn't have to be killed for maybe another year. But her milk had started to emit a new-car smell, which was becoming common with the two-udder cows. So she had to die. He was the one that made that rule after all.

As My Best Friend approached, Farmer Ted 1 wondered aloud if she knew she was about to be turned off like a light switch. Surprisingly, she answered by transmitting a psychic message to everyone within a 140-meter radius: "You may kill our bodies, but our quest to get as weird as possible will continue forever."

This was not simply a last bovine broadcast. It was a cow curse made possible due to the experimental chemical injections used to grow the extra udder. It was an unexpected side effect. Additional research was needed to determine just how the chemical gave My Best Friend the ability to utilize black magic. Another observed side effect was that the cows had gained the ability to play a version of the game of leapfrog: Leapfrog Cow.

Now, finally, Farmer Ted 2 was witnessing these cow shenanigans with his own two eyes. But, seemingly out of the blue, Farmer Ted 1 chose this time to demand that Farmer Ted 2 make him a BLT with avocado on lightly toasted pumpernickel bread. This wasn't actually that surprising, as he'd been ordering Farmer Ted 2 to make this exact sandwich on demand every day since they were children. But performing this task now meant that Farmer Ted 2 would be denied the opportunity of watching Farmer Ted 1 slaughter Farmer Ted 1's best friend. The cruelty continued in a never-ending loop.

Farmer Ted 1 gave My Best Friend one last kiss on both of her udders, blew a booger out of his right nostril, and then shot her in the head with his brand-new bolt gun, a birthday gift from Old Man "Mongoose" McGeester. Every single cow in the underground farm immediately stopped playing Leapfrog Cow. It was as if they were being controlled by the same cow mind. This same behavior was reported in all the other underground farms across the United States of America.

A flag displaying a picture of My Best Friend in the style of a dopey 1980s double-exposure yearbook portrait was hung at half-staff, and the fake underground sun was slowly dimmed for dramatic effect.

✎✐ THE BIRTH OF THE PANTS OF INSANITY ✐✎

The cowhide was suspended from rocking frames and dumped into a series of vats holding various chemical solutions until it started to look like leather. The process was unexpectedly interesting and visually pleasing. The leather hide's journey continued through a rolling machine and into a rotating drum, where it was rolled in oils and greases. It traveled through a series of drying tunnels until, finally, it was brushed under a revolving brush-covered cylinder. The finished leather was placed on top of a pattern in the shape of a pant design and then cut precisely by a machine's blade.

A seamstress made the final stitch in the pair of leather pants, and they were laid flat on the table. And THEN THE PANTS BEGAN TO GLOW—A DARK PASTEL GREEN. The freaked-out seamstress sprinted out of the sweatshop and ran straight into the guard at the factory door. The seamstress was escorted back to her work spot, where she pretended to calm down, folded the leather pants, and put them on top of a pile of duplicate leather pants.

Chapter Two

Meet the Pants

The leather pants had now made it to the final stage: dangling from a hanger at the Keytar Clothing and Pipe Shop. Yes, there was a keytar-shaped pinball machine. Yes, there was a keytar-shaped jukebox. Yes, there were keytar-shaped pipes for sale. Yes, there was a keytar for sale.

Standing directly in front of the pants was Mr. Taffle, a 19-year-old man-child who had been called *almost handsome* by several women who had no connection to each other. Of course, on none of those occasions had he been wearing his dorky plastic headband from which dangled a miniature camera in front of his face. He also had not been wearing his pea-green polyester suit (with only one leg properly hemmed), nor had he been nervously pinching his left nipple.

Mr. Taffle stared at the pants with a hypnotic confusion that kept morphing into passionate intrigue. He needed something really special to wear to the annual Mighty Warlord Extravaganza—something that would make him stand out just ever so slightly above the rest of the salesmen, without looking like he was trying. But these leather pants were obviously out of the question... Or were they?

Mr. Taffle looked away, but his eyes immediately came back to the pants. He looked away again... and right back at them. Why was this so hard?

He finally managed to pry his eyes away and proceed down the aisle of flashy clothes. Perhaps a straight striped leisure suit would work... but not as well as those leather pants. As if being pulled by a gigantic magnet strong enough to tow a man (albeit one with little-boy muscles), Mr. Taffle quickly returned to the pants.

While he could clearly intellectualize about how bizarre this obsession with the pants was, he also realized that he had to touch them—RIGHT NOW.

However, just as Mr. Taffle reached out to finger the pants, the robotic *Snobby Royalty English Accent* female voice from his phone snapped him out of his trance. "Mr. Taffle, you must leave immediately in order to be ten minutes early." Even though this pre-selected voice came from the *Never Be Late* app, it seemed suspiciously timed to keep him from touching those pants. And not even the bizarre, intoxicating allure of them could induce him to be late to anything ever again. "No way. Not going to happen. Ever."

As he made a beeline for the exit, turning around for one final look at the pants, he slammed smack into the front counter. He suddenly found himself face to face with the shop's owner.

Leonardo Pierre Le Rat Vissoir was dressed in a sparkly gold double-breasted jacket with flying saucer-shaped shoulder blades. He wore gold vinyl glow wristbands, and he had gold spiked hair. "Le Rat" classified this style as Serge Gainsbourg from the year 2171. He would tell this to all the customers, fully aware that most Americans didn't know who Serge Gainsbourg was, even though they would pretend to. Watching people lie was fun.

Vissior was known to most people simply as "Le Rat" because of the hot pink and gold-striped "Le Rat" neck tattoo he claimed he had gotten because of a bet that he had "won, yes won." In fact, he had gotten this tattoo only a day before he had escaped to the United States of America, where he quickly opened up the keytar shop. Le Rat thought that if he surrounded himself with keytars, he would finally be motivated to learn how to play his dream instrument. But tragically, no matter how hard he practiced, he totally sucked at the keytar. And he was now surrounded every day by his suckiness. This made him very cranky and homesick. Oh, how he longed to return to gay Paree. If only there weren't so many sociopaths there obsessed with collecting the money and jewels he owed them.

Le Rat glared at Mr. Taffle, then rotated his nostrils in a freakily spastic way. Mr. Taffle didn't know what this action meant, but for some reason it felt like it was possibly the most disrespectful thing anyone had ever done to him. Should he say something to this snobby, futuristic, intriguing jerk? No, he was late. Plus, he was a coward.

Mr. Taffle walked up to the front of Mr. Winkie Electronics corporate headquarters, which was considered the most modern office building in the world. (Actually, halfway through construction, the Mr. Winkie Corporate Espionage Division discovered it would have been just the *second* most modern building in the world. So construction was halted to install the proper upgrades, including removing all the corners of the building, so they could once again claim the top spot.)

The inside of the building had a fun we-never-want-you-to-leave-work-so-enjoy-our-fluff-and-fold-laundry-just-past-the-Poke-bar-but-if-you-pass-the-deep-tissue-massage-and-myofascial-clinic-you've-gone-too-far kind of vibe. The flashing Mr. Winkie Electronics logo (Mr. Winkie's sweaty, joyful face) greeted each visitor in every direction one could possibly turn. This wasn't intentionally designed to be creepy as hell.

Mr. Taffle entered his transparent bubble cubicle, just one of the 243 other transparent bubble cubicles on the floor. This design guaranteed that each worker could be seen from any angle, all the time. In addition, a hidden scanner ray would monitor each employee every 15 minutes to determine how hard they were really working. It had been proven that such a work environment caused productivity to rise 19%—although everyone in the company was told to say it rose to 20%.

Advanced-metric Moneyball analytics were utilized to decide that every employee should be called by Mr. or Ms., with no first names used. Actually, this part was determined using some fuzzy math, but Mr. Winkie was so psyched about his "Mr. and Ms." idea that the corporate statistical team was awarded bonus sick days simply for doing what he wanted without asking questions.

Mr. Taffle's computer turned on the moment he sat down. It was Pleebley Weebly time. Mr. Taffle knew this because his computer screen announced, in flashing graphics, *It's Pleebley Weebly Time!* Instantly, the excited, fresh-out-of-community-college face of the potential Pleebley Weebly—Mr. Lopez (also wearing one of the camera headbands)—appeared on the screen.

"Good afternoon, Mr. Lopez. I'm so very pleased you received your Mr. Winkie Projecto headband," said Mr. Taffle, followed by a playful eyebrow shuffle. "Are you ready for your mind to be blown?"

"Um, okay," said Mr. Lopez with a careful smile.

"Well, just push that Mr. Winkie icon you downloaded on your phone and…"

A two-foot hologram of Mr. Lopez's face appeared in front of Mr. Taffle from out of his miniature camera.

"This is amazeballs!" Mr. Lopez shouted, with dribbles of hologram spit flying. "Is the hologram of my face right in front of your face like yours is right in front of my face?!"

"Yes, your very unexcited hologram is right in front of me," playfully teased Mr. Taffle. "But this isn't the big surprise. *This* is…!" Mr. Taffle poked Mr. Lopez's projection.

"I totally felt that poke! Unbelievable!"

"You felt it because you just experienced Feel Technology. Mr. Winkie Electronics is the only company in the world to possess this groundbreaking know-how," said Mr. Taffle with a sneaky but steady uptick of enthusiasm. "We're also embarking on a groundbreaking marketing campaign that involves building a virtual sales army to take over the real and virtual world. I'm telling you all this, Mr. Lopez, because I think you would be an ideal candidate for the Mr. Winkie Electronic Global Army and Family."

"I can't believe I'm interested. Oh, I'm sorry; that sounded a bit rude."

"Not at all. Let me transfer your projection to the Projecto headband of Mr. Manley, my team leader. I know he'll be just as impressed with you as I am. And from the bottom of my heart, I'm so psyched we'll soon be colleagues, joking about *the life discount*."

"Life discount, huh?" Mr. Lopez asked a tad suspiciously, which read loud and clear that this Pleebley Weebly was now *free fallin' like*

Tom Petty, yo. So Mr. Taffle dug deep into the techniques taught by his mentor Mr. Manley regarding sales *free fallin' like Tom Petty, yo,* where he would emphasize that the sales game was all about *learning to fly like Tom Petty, yo.*

"Oh, *'life discount'* is just our clever nickname for the sliding commission scale. We'll have some laughs about that later when I take you out to your celebratory dinner at a Brazilian steakhouse that utilizes the century-old cooking techniques of churrasco," chimed Mr. Taffle with a smile that looked as if he were opening his mouth wide for the dentist.

"Oh, I get it now. You're like a carny, pitching the townsfolk a magical elixir from the back of your gypsy horse carriage," calmly stated Mr. Lopez as he extended his middle finger. "Why don't you feel this?" Mr. Lopez wiggled his middle finger a few times before his projection disappeared.

"Nooooooooooo!" Mr. Taffle buried his headband camera in his hairless chest. How was he going to explain this to Mr. Manley?

The only thing that had gone his way in the last year was when Mr. Manley picked him to ride under his wing. But now he was going to have to face the music. He hoisted his head up painfully until his upper lip was perfectly aligned with the flashing mustache blinking on his computer screen. Mr. Taffle pressed the pixilated mustache with the tip of his nose, and the projection of Mr. Manley's face (with a mustache/man-perm combo that Mr. Manley constantly described as *next level macho*) appeared in front of Mr. Taffle. Mr. Manley immediately knew something was wrong. He looked genuinely concerned.

"Your almost-handsome face tells me that you're wondering why I blew you off when I was clearly supposed to help you pick an outfit for the Mighty Warlord Extravaganza," said Mr. Manley with the kind of joyful smile that read loud and clear that he was mocking you. "Well... wait for it... wait for it... it's because I was extremely busy doing nothing. And then, just like that, here we are, Mr. Taffle. That's called magic."

"That's not really what I'm upset about," sheepishly mumbled Mr. Taffle, basically to himself. It was clear that Mr. Manley wasn't listening; he was already thinking about what to say next.

"I would have gladly assisted you in picking out some sick power threads so you don't look all baffoony-like tomorrow night. But let's not forget that my "The Treehouse" is right near the Keytar Clothing and Pipes Shop. You probably would have just come over and gotten me, had you been clued in on a little something we in the know like to call *initiative*. I want you to think about that right..." Mr. Manley carefully counted to 11 seconds in his head, "... NOW."

Mr. Taffle tilted his right eyebrow up like Mr. Spock of the starship *Enterprise* to let Mr. Manley know he was seriously think-ing hard, despite the fact that Mr. Manley was the one who had taught him this top-10 facial manipulation technique.

"Okay, enough jibber-jabber. Projecto me over to your Pleebley Weebly," ordered Mr. Manley.

"That's what's wrong. I lost my Pleebley Weebly," admitted Mr. Taffle under his breath. "I don't know what happened. One minute he was so excited, and then the next, he thought I was trying to con him."

"Hey, that's the sales game. Even a four-time Mighty Warlord—hey, that's me and me and me and me—has had that happen to them before. No, it hasn't. I'm lying to you. But let me now be as honest with you as I'm contractually obligated. There's only one thing holding you back from making a big impression here in the sales division of Mr. Winkie Electronics."

"Thank you. I'm listening," said a grateful Mr. Taffle.

"Now, according to the principles of math-e-matics... you totally suck. You're also very crappy at sales. But you can solve this problem if you..." teased Mr. Manley, inserting a dramatic rising-tension the-theater-is-listening hum before continuing, "...stop sucking right away. Mr. Taffle, I care about you because I'm your mentor. I've also been recorded guaranteeing that I could turn even the biggest loser employee into something that was at least borderline passable."

"Well, let's pray for a miracle that the sucking will end, because I have a meeting today with the President of Monetary Financial regarding using the Projecto headbands for all their teleconference meetings around the world."

Mr. Manley looked extremely impressed, making it difficult to tell if he was mocking Mr. Taffle or not. "Well, look at you, with the big-time macho manly manpower move. How in the world did you hook a glazed mackerel?"

Mr. Taffle really wanted to lie, but he would never lie about anything unless he thought someone would punch him the face if he told the truth.

"I hooked the glazed mackerel because he owes... my mother a favor."

Mr. Manley rotated his head in a full slow-motion counter-clockwise circle. He then spun his head in a full clockwise circle, as if he was being fast-forwarded on high. He repeated both these head rotations four more times, his breathing getting deeper on each rotation, before finally shouting, "THANKS, MRS. TAFFLE! YOU'RE THE BEST MOMMY EVERRRRRRRRRR!"

CHAPTER THREE

Sizzle, Sizzle, Sizzle

r. Taffle walked down the street as if a piece of toilet paper was stuck up his butt, because it was. He would often get distracted when he was nervous and turn extra stupid. At least he had remembered to zip up his fly this time. *Always focus on the positive to start sizzling.* As he approached the intimidating 122 floors of the Monetary Financial Corporate Tower, he thought of... those leather pants? This was the most important business meeting of his life, and he couldn't stop thinking about how good he might look in those pants. Why?!

As Mr. Taffle approached the desk of the almost-retired female Monetary Financial Corporate executive assistant, he noticed she had lipstick on her teeth. He decided it would be best not to mention it, but she sensed that he had noticed something. Then she saw in the reflection of her computer screen the magenta streak across her teeth. So now she blamed him, as if he was somehow responsible. It was like a sonic burst of pure hatred had been shot into her brain. It made her feel tingly.

"Hello, I'm Mr. Taffle, and I have a meeting with Mr. Ziska. I'm actually 15 minutes early, but I'm always early," chuckled Mr. Taffle, with his best charming grin.

But it didn't matter. The Monetary Financial Corporate executive assistant now hated him to an unnatural extent. She checked her computer, saw he wasn't lying about the appointment, and felt the all-too-familiar sting of disappointment. However, the appointment came with additional interesting meeting notes.

"Says here that Mr. Ziska owes your frisky mother, and she's been annoying him about it," she read while taking her right finger and wiping the lipstick off her teeth. "Look, I've been Mr. Ziska's executive assistant for 16 years, and if there is one piece of advice I can grant you, it is..."

She stopped. "No, I'm not going to. How's my lipstick?"

"I told you to reschedule!" screamed Mr. Ziska at Mr. Taffle. Mr. Ziska was a middle-aged man who was infatuated with lifting weights only slightly less than he was with taking steroids.

The mahogany walls of Mr. Ziska's mahogany-everything office were filled with pictures of him posing and lifting weights with other people who also enjoyed taking steroids. The Monetary Financial Corporate executive assistant couldn't help but smirk, hearing the news about the rescheduling. She would now get to personally escort Mr. Taffle out of the building. When they were in the elevator together, she would insist he never look her directly in the eye. She loved that part so much. It made her feel like prime Madonna.

Mr. Ziska saw the joyful look on the Monetary Financial Corporate executive assistant's face, which caused him to immediately reverse his decision. He suspected that making her happy was the reason he had broken out with a hideous case of bacne.

"Ahhhhh, that's okay, I guess I'll see Mr. Taffle now, sighed Mr. Ziska, bordering on creepy. "His mother did do that thing for me, after all."

"Splendid. I'll go get you your coffee, sir," said the Monetary Financial Corporate executive assistant, as she stormed out of the office.

"So, how's your talented mother?" asked Mr. Ziska.

"My mother is fine, thank you," said Mr. Taffle, hoping they would not have to talk about his mother.

"She has an amazing knack for doing the right thing," said Mr. Ziska with a blatantly inappropriate smile.

"I'm not sure I know what you mean," replied Mr. Taffle in an inquisitive tone that in no way suggested any hostility of a son wondering if another man besides their daddy had made love to their mommy.

"Alright, you've got five minutes. What do you got for me?" asked Mr. Ziska, already feeling bored from the anticipation of being bored.

"What I got for you is a REVOLUTION," said Mr. Taffle with a loud snap of his fingers, "in the way Monetary Financial will communicate around the world."

Mr. Ziska slowly lowered his head, drifting into a dream that involved Mrs. Taffle injecting him with steroids.

"How would you like to slap someone on the other side of the world in the face?"

Mr. Ziska pepped right up. "Okay, I'm intrigued. Show me, Mr. Taffle."

Mr. Taffle whipped out a Mr. Winkie Projecto headband from his jacket's inside pocket. "There's your life before Projecto, and then there's your life after Projecto. Are you sure you're ready for this?" taunted Mr. Taffle in a cheeseball way that miraculously came off as endearing. "Now, download the Mr. Winkie app on your phone and turn away from me. Then, when it's loaded, press the Mr. Winkie icon."

Mr. Ziska obeyed all of Mr. Taffle's instructions. He giggled in delight as Mr. Taffle's projection appeared in front of Mr. Ziska's face.

"So, you're telling me that I can smack your projection in the face, and you can actually feel it?" asked Mr. Ziska.

"That's right. It's called "Feel" Technology, and we here at—"

WHAP!

"Ouch," said Mr. Taffle.

"You really can feel that!" he cheered, as the steroids in his bloodstream tickled his brain.

"Yes, sir. Now, just imagine how communication around the world can be—"

WHAP! WHAP! WHAP! WHAP! WHAP! WHAP! WHAP! WHAP! WHAP!

"This is the most amazing thing ever created!" screamed Mr. Ziska as he continued slapping Mr. Taffle. "I want every analyst at Monetary Financial Worldwide to wear a Projecto AT ALL TIMES!"

There was no way some computerized slapping pain was going to keep Mr. Taffle from pulling this glazed mackerel into the butter Jacuzzi. This would be by far the greatest sale in the history of Mr. Winkie.

"Everyone at Mr. Winkie is prepping to go into the monthly meeting. But my team leader, Mr. Manley, will call you—or should

I say, Projecto you—first thing right after," declared Mr. Taffle with the confidence of a future Mighty Warlord.

"You tell this Mr. Manley I'll be ready for him," replied Mr. Ziska, as he threw one final flying elbow to the throat of Mr. Taffle's projection.

"Ouch," said Mr. Taffle.

Mr. Taffle strutted down the Monetary Financial Corporate hallway like someone who had never strutted before. It looked like he had cramps in both his legs. This caused a medium-sized piece of toilet paper that had been stuck inside of his improperly hemmed pant leg to slide out and onto the Monetary Financial Corporate surf-and-sand executive carpet. Mr. Taffle nonchalantly walked back, picked up the toilet paper, and stuck it in his jacket pocket.

He turned back around, smacking right into the Monetary Financial Corporate executive assistant, who was holding a piping hot oversized mug of a coffee labeled "Big Z". The coffee exploded all over them, but the majority landed on the Monetary Financial Corporate executive assistant. She yelped like a wounded bobcat.

"Oh, my God! I'm so sorry!" exclaimed Mr. Taffle.

"I hate everything about you!" snapped the Monetary Financial Corporate executive assistant.

"Ummmm, I have to go or I'm going to be late, and I'm never ever late. But I'll send you money for dry cleaning ASAP!" called back Mr. Taffle as he scurried to the elevator.

The Mr. Winkie conference room was built in a castle design, stadium style. It contained the jousting-themed restaurant Medieval Times, which had a seating capacity of 1,500. The computer had found a statistical data anomaly showing that eating utensil-free meals in a castle-like space during the Shock and Awe marketing sessions increased the sales staff's ability to manipulate by a whopping 43%. So, all employees were encouraged to bring their own game hens and turkey drumsticks to consume and chuck on the ground during meetings, with the caveat that the worst salesman of the month would have to clean up all the bones after the meeting. It was such a humiliating task that there never was a repeat worst salesman of the month in the history of the Mr. Winkie's War Room Weekly Wag-a-thon. This was cause for a lot of fist bumps at the bi-weekly upper middle management themed cocktail hours.

Ms. Branch, with both arms covered in Tribute to Wall Street tattoo sleeves that stuck out of the rolled-up sleeves of her pantsuit, stood in the middle of the conference stadium punching herself in both of her padded shoulders. She had recently been promoted to lead Wag-a-thon, and she credited Mr. Manley's teachings as one of the reasons for her rapid advancement.

"Watching someone get psyched up is an easy way to trick other people into getting psyched up," Mr. Manley had stated at the Mr. Winkie Executive Retreat, while leading a game featuring beanbags and buckets of ice-cold water.

Ms. Branch lifted her head up dramatically, causing the 1,500 members of the Mr. Winkie Electronic Global Army and Family— all wearing their own Projecto headbands—to hiss a volcanic, "SIZZZZZZZZLE."

"WE DON'T STOP FOR LUNCH," chanted Ms. Branch.

"'CAUSE LUNCH IS FOR CHUMPS," returned the Mr. Winkie sales team.

This call-and-response ping-pong chanting game continued.

"WE SELL ALL THE TIME!"

"'CAUSE FREE TIME'S A CRIME!"

"WE ALWAYS REHASH?!"

"TO DOUBLE OUR CASH"

"WE'LL BARGE RIGHT IN"

"INCREASING THEM MARGINS."

Mr. Taffle, with a coffee stain perfectly centered on his shirt, and Mr. Manley sat in Row G, seats 49 and 50, for the meeting. These were considered the best seats in the house. This was one of the perks of being under the mentorship of a Mighty Warlord like Mr. Manley.

"Frankly, Mr. Taffle, because of the new-fangled reality that you just hooked the glazed mackerel, I'm being bombarded with existential questions from the gang of rascals squatting in my forehead," whispered Mr. Manley into Mr. Taffle's ear.

"How did you know?" asked a surprised Mr. Taffle at the exact same time as Mr. Manley answered, "That hilarious coffee stain can't hide your eye of the tiger, which is also the theme song to the third film in the *Rocky* saga, which coincidentally starred Mr. T— which, coincidentally, is what I call you when I'm too lazy to say the entire Mr. T... affle. But Mr. T... affle, perhaps I should now call you the Mr. Dark Horse candidate to be ..." And as if Ms. Branch was somehow listening to their conversation, she chanted perfectly in unison with Mr. Manley, "to be crowned the MIGHTY..."

"WARLORD!"

"MIGHTY!"

"WARLORD!"

"SIZZLE! SIZZLE! SIZZLE! SIZZLE! SIZZLE! SIZZLE!"

"Now, for the first time, we are going to be Projectoed all around the world," she exclaimed enthusiastically, and then busted into the 360-degree spin she had been practicing all year. "So, I'd recommend coming at least 45 minutes before showtime so you can fully enjoy the all-you-can-eat buffet and open bar until 6:45. But first, I'd like to steer this meeting off-road and share with you some unbelievable news I just received. I spoke with the president of Monetary Financial, who informed me that he has agreed in principle on a deal to purchase enough Projectos to make it the biggest single order in the history of Mr. Winkie Electronics. So, I'd like us to give up some major-league *SIZZLE* for MR. TAFFLE! Now, get down here, you Big Champ, and receive your *sizzle!*"

Mr. Taffle couldn't believe it. He was going to become a Big Champ. This was the greatest moment of his Mr. Winkie existence, easily beating the time he'd gotten paid for coming in on a Sunday.

SURROUND-SOUND *SIZZLES!*

Mr. Taffle air-galloped on top of an air donkey down to center stage. This was a Big Champ tradition. He exchanged fierce high fives with the Mr. Winkie sales force that lined the aisle as he galloped past them. A senior sales manager named Ms. Rucker even handed him her turkey drumstick, which he carefully nibbled on for the rest of the air-donkey ride down.

Mr. Taffle reached center stage and immediately was air-lassoed in by Ms. Branch. Ms. Branch, with a proud grin, extended her hand for a Big Champ high five... but then abruptly pulled her hand away and slapped her butt hard. The salesman frenzy immediately stopped.

"Let me tell you what happened after Mr. Taffle left the president's office," announced Ms. Branch. "Turns out he crushed a full 40-ounce cup of scalding hot coffee on the brand-new blouse of the president's executive assistant of 16 years. Now the deal is... (in Mr. Taffle's ear) "KAAAAAAAAAABOOOOOM!"

(Back to the salesmen) "... not going to happen anymore. But the deal wouldn't have..."

(In Mr. Taffle's ear) "KAAAAPLOOOOOOOOOOOOOOWED!"

(Back to the salesman) "... failed if Mr. Taffle had followed the proper procedure and had his team leader and four-time Mighty Warlord Mr. Manley on the phone, closing the deal like a pro, before Mr. Taffle had a chance to..."

(In Mr. Taffle's ear) "KAAAAAAAAAAABAAAAAAASHED!"

(Back to the salesman) "… destroy the deal. So, instead of being a big champ, Mr. Taffle is now a big CHUMP!"

The salesmen all flapped their arms like the large chomping jaws of a swarm of gators in a feeding frenzy.

"CHUMP! CHUMP! CHUMP! CHUMP! CHUMP! CHUMP! CHUMP! CHUMP!"

Chapter Four

The Good, The Bad, And Le Rat

Mr. Taffle sat, parked in his beige Volvo, staring intently at the steering wheel that possessed an air bag system that made Volvo the safest automobile in the world. This was the reason he was leasing one. He was so tired of sucking really bad at everything in the world. It was embarrassing.

But he wasn't just going to go home, curl up in the fetal position on his faux-fur saucer chair while watching *Jeopardy* and realizing he was one level too stupid to ever be a contestant on *Jeopardy*, and then eating the pain away even if it meant busting into his apocalypse rations and eating all the dried apricots again.

Mr. Taffle wanted to feel the power of the *sizzle,* like, so bad. Almost as bad as he wanted those leather pants. And now was the time to at least check *that* box.

When he heard Mr. Taffle charge into the Keytar Clothing and Pipe Store, Le Rat painfully pried his eyes away from his erotic Napoleon-centered romance novel. "Piss, piss, piss," Le Rat whisper hissed at Mr. Taffle.

But Mr. Taffle didn't hear a thing. He was locked in on the leather pants. He made a beeline for them, yanked them off the rack, and charged up to the register with his head down.

"Excuse me, sir. I'd like to try on these pants, please," said Mr. Taffle, with his head still down.

Le Rat pretended he didn't hear him, immediately jogging to the furthest possible corner of the store. He pressed his face against the wall and held his breath. Before Mr. Taffle could even begin to weigh the pros and cons of confronting Le Rat for this over-the-top diss, an over-the-top suspense movie jingle interrupted.

The projection of Mr. Taffle's mom's face—a 40-year-old wearing a little too much makeup, which was meant to hide how much she liked to party—appeared out of the Projecto camera.

"Hi, honey. I'm just totally dying to know how your meeting went with Big Z?" his mother asked excitedly. "I mean Mr. Ziska. I'm just used to calling him Big Z because that always makes him purr like a malnourished kitten, and I've become sort of addicted to that. Sorry, I know, too much information."

Mr. Taffle had *no idea what she was talking about*—at least that's what he told himself.

"Well, it went great," he said, to his mother's absolute delight. "And then, it went pretty much the worst it could possibly have gone."

"You didn't accidentally stroke him in the back of his right upper thigh?" she asked nervously.

"No," said Mr. Taffle. He decided he was going to think of piglets playing with panda bears anytime he had suspicions of any hanky-panky between his mother and Mr. Ziska. "It's just that, according to my mentor Mr. Manley, I suck."

"Now, I highly doubt that such an esteemed employee like Mr. Manley would agree to be your mentor if you didn't have at least some kind of potential," she said in the same sweet motherly tone she used to get out of the *accidental* shoplifting incident at Romantixxx. Mr. Taffle took his mother's words in deep.

"You're right, Mother. I'm just going to keep working harder and harder and harder until I don't suck. And I'm not going to stop until I'm crowned the Mighty Warlord."

Mrs. Taffle's projection leaned in close and switched from sweet motherly tone to wise motherly tone. "Honey, I'm so proud of how hard you're working. But you've got to understand that some people were meant to be Mighty Warlords and some were meant to eventually decide they should go to dental school. And there's nothing wrong with that. Nothing at all."

Mr. Taffle tried to hide his anger.

"I need to be… better. I used to be better. I was way better a year and a half ago…"

Mrs. Taffle knew exactly what the *year and a half ago* incident was, as she had since tried to avoid talking about it with him every day for a year and a half.

"Look, deary. I'm very aware of your feelings. But a girl like Katrina most likely was a one-time deal. And that's okay. Trust me. It'll make it much easier to succeed in business when your head isn't constantly stuck in the lovey-dovey clouds. Big Z taught me that."

"I've got to go now if I'm going to keep on schedule," he interjected, as piglets and panda bears pirouetted inside his head. "I still have to pick out an outfit for the Mighty Warlord Extravaganza tomorrow."

Mrs. Taffle's motherly smile transformed into one of grave concern. "You should strongly consider having someone else pick out the outfit for you, honey."

"I've got it covered. Got to go."

"Okay then. Have a wonderful day, darling. Just try to remember that you don't totally suck. And for God's sake, whatever you do, please don't pick out that outfit by yourself. Love you to pieces. Don't do it." Mr. Taffle's mother's projection gave Mr. Taffle a kiss and then disappeared.

Mr. Taffle couldn't help but stew on the memory of Katrina every time "a year and a half ago" was brought up. She was so perfect in all the ways extremely hot people are when they actually want to go out with someone way beneath them and have no obvious self-esteem issues. But it wasn't just superficial. They had a magical bond, which included how passionately they loved to learn, despite neither ever having been described as "bright." They had invented a game called "Blow Your Mind," where they would try to one-up each other with who could find the most incredible fun fact. The game would get so intense that Mr. Taffle could almost stop constantly thinking about making out with her. Plus, they just enjoyed the hell out of being nice to each other. They were literally always smiling—lots of giggling, ice cream, museums, and tickling attacks. It was all love, love, love, love, love, love—and then... BRICK WALL. No warning. It was just over without explanation. He was told not to contact her by her little brother Little Melvin. So he agreed, even though he suspected that Little Melvin might be lying and also that he might be the spawn of Satan.

Mr. Taffle marched up to Le Rat, whose face had grown purplish pink from holding his breath in the corner. "I would like to try on these pants, please!"

Le Rat exhaled like a punctured whoopee cushion while stating painfully slow, "You do not need help with those pants."

"You're right. I don't need your help to try them on. Thank you," Mr. Taffle said as he walked backwards to the changing room, his eyes locked on Le Rat the entire time.

Mr. Taffle removed his faded chocolate brown Hush Puppies, revealing his socks (orange with pea green polka dots). He then peeled off his pea green pants and stood in just his green underwear. A tiny yellow stain on his crotch gave off a lemon/lime vibe.

Mr. Taffle slid on the leather pants and did a 360°, checking out his reflection in the changing-room mirror. Damn, his butt looked solid. And then, for a brief moment, he thought he saw the pants glowing a dark pastel green. Before he could even process whether he had just imagined the glow, a machine-gun barrage of knocks came from the other side of the door.

"Let me see how the pants look on you," demanded Le Rat.

This confused Mr. Taffle profoundly. On the one hand, there would be some satisfaction of showing off how amazing he looked in the pants. It would also grant his mother's wish of having someone sign off on his fashion selection. But then he remembered Le Rat's rude nostril rotation from earlier.

"No thank you sir!"

"Bock. Bock. Bock... BOCK!" clucked Le Rat with a realistic chicken cluck that could fool most chickens.

Oh, if you think that's going to work, well, that's where you're right. Besides I know I look hot as hell in these babies, thought Mr. Taffle, as he swung open the changing room door to reveal himself.

One look at Mr. Taffle, and Le Rat struggled to keep his balance. He looked like a man who couldn't take it anymore, whatever *it* was.

"Please, I'm begging you not to purchase these pants," said Le Rat. This was followed by a strange grunt and some left nostril rotation. Oh, how Mr. Taffle loathed this nostril rotation.

"Actually, I *am* going to buy them, sir. Thank you," Mr. Taffle smirked. Just then he realized that he hadn't yet looked at the price tag. It didn't matter. He was all in no matter what. Mr. Taffle and Le Rat glared at each other, both doing their best spaghetti western stare-down until it got awkward.

"But first, I'm going to change back into my suit. So, give me a moment, please. Thank you."

Le Rat went back to reading his book and waited for Mr. Taffle behind the cash register. He was over being terrified and was already back to his usual look of snobby-cool-meets-eccentric-with-a-dash-of-mischief. Mr. Taffle finally glanced at the pants' price tag. They were $550 before tax.

The only time Mr. Taffle had spent $550 on anything non-automobile-related was never. The combined total of all the clothes he had bought since his parents had stopped buying them for him was $309, including tax. But these pants needed to be his— and, he thought, that's what credit cards are for.

Mr. Taffle slammed his American Express down hard on the counter, a bit surprised by his aggressiveness. This action immediately induced more nostril rotation from Le Rat. The two continued to stare at each other while they waited for the credit card transaction to be approved. Meantime, Le Rat whistled the theme from *The Good, the Bad and the Ugly* as masterfully as he had done his chicken clucks. Finally he spoke.

"You think this has ended. But believe Leonardo Pierre Le Rat Vissoir when he says that this has really just begun," ominously warned Le Rat, who only revealed his full name when he was dead serious or when he was at the DMV.

With his eyes still focused on Mr. Taffle, Le Rat ripped off the credit card receipt and slid it over to Mr. Taffle. Mr. Taffle didn't remove his own eyes from Le Rat as he signed "Mr. Taffle" on the receipt, five inches above the signature line.

The English woman from his phone interrupted.

"You need to leave now in order to be 10 minutes early."

Mr. Taffle walked out of the store with the smile of someone who believed they had won something, though actually they had just spent their weekly salary on a pair of pants they would most likely never wear.

CHAPTER FIVE

Loosey Goosey

As Mr. Taffle drove home, he couldn't help but take a few sneak peeks at the pants in the bag.

"Wow, they're just so cool... Just one more little looky... And just one more." He glanced up barely in time to break for an octogenarian lady crossing in the middle of the street, struggling to push her shopping cart. Should he pull over and help, thus risking being late for the first time since he vowed never to be late again?

Noooooooyeeessss.

Mr. Taffle pushed the octogenarian's cart across the street, but her snail's pace decreased as they progressed. She was excited that anyone not being paid by the government would let her talk at them.

"You always hear about strawberry and raspberry and blueberry, but you barely ever hear about boysenberry," huffed the octogenarian, as she stopped in the middle of the street. "And it pisses me off!"

"You're right. You really don't hear much about boysenberry."

"Miniaturized Vikings stole my magnetic ring and anti-inflammatory supplements."

Traffic backed up seven cars deep waiting for them, all eyes glaring at Mr. Taffle as if he were responsible.

"We should really keep walking, ma'am."

"Don't tell me what to do, dork. I tell *you* what to do," she said as she flicked Mr. Taffle in the left eyeball.

"You need to leave right now, or you will be one minute late," warned the English woman on his phone.

"Tell that limey lass in your pocket you're currently spoken for," ordered the octogenarian.

Mr. Taffle had often pondered whether invisible sound waves, similar to the ones that let whales communicate with each other, were somehow being emitted from his brain. This could explain what caused so many people to hate him so deeply for no apparent reason. It was just a theory, but it kept coming up.

Mr. Taffle drove his Volvo toward his home faster than he had ever driven (62 miles per hour in a 55-mph zone), all the while being taunted by the English woman on his phone.

"Why did you even download this app if you wanted to be late? Stop lying to yourself, you scared little insecure manboy." Mr. Taffle hadn't realized there was a snarky setting on the Never Be Late app that could be lowered or turned off completely.

Mr. Taffle sped up to his sprawling apartment complex, Rosemary Ridge, which was essentially a half- mile long stretch of identical box-shaped living quarters stacked on top of each other.

Rosemary Ridge's calling card was that the complex was surrounded by the greenest grass. It had been treated with the most powerful chemicals that may or may not be safe, as environmental regulations had been removed as part of pork belly legislation that had been tacked on to an amendment that would put seatbelts on school buses.

Rosemary Ridge coincidentally used the same statistical analysis team used by Mr. Winkie Electronics. This team had projected that occupancy would rise 44% with the inclusion of the extreme green grass, thus easily offsetting any fees and penalties incurred from future lawsuits concerning odd things happening to renters' flesh.

Mr. Taffle, with the clothing bag swinging like a drunk cowboy's lasso, stormed into his apartment, scooped the remote control off the top off his coffee table, and turned on his wall-mounted 52" flat screen television. He leaped perfectly into his faux-fur saucer chair just as the theme music for *Jeopardy* started. He'd made it!

Mr. Taffle threw his arms up in victory and then kicked out his legs, which caused the oversized Jenga tower on the coffee table to topple over. Even Mr. Taffle would have to admit that, if anyone knew that all of his rushing to be 10 minutes early was just so he wouldn't miss the start of *Jeopardy*, it would be pretty annoying to most people. But if they also knew that he had been rushing so he could watch a rerun he had already seen multiple times and which he himself had programmed to start at the traditional 6:30 PM start time, then that would be considered pretty annoying to everyone on earth.

Mr. Taffle also had a tradition while watching *Jeopardy* to shout the answers at his television. Sometimes he would lie to himself about knowing the answer and simply repeat it as the contestant was answering, with a half-second lag time. However, most of the time he just focused on remembering the *Jeopardy* answers as fun facts to bust out at all the Mr. Winkie sales mixers and hazing sessions.

As Contestant 1, a sickly-looking Indian man with a patchy goatee, asked, "Let's go for Famous Love Poems for $400." Mr. Taffle knew that considering the subject of love would guarantee that Katrina would soon invade his thoughts again in the usual *wing zang zoom* montage way.

A young Alex Trebek—who, according to Mr. Manley's spreadsheet, was ranked the 11th greatest former macho mustache man with a top-rated man perm—read the answer.

"I told my love, I told my love. I told her all my heart. Trembling, cold, in ghastly fears. Ah! She did depart...is from the poem *Love's Secret* by this poet?"

Holy crap, Mr. Taffle actually remembered this one.

"Who is Walt Whitman?!" shouted Mr. Taffle.

"Who is William Blake?" said Contestant 1.

"And you are correct," said Alex Trebek.

"GOD-DARN-IT!"

As soon as his show ended, Mr. Taffle slid on his Projecto headband and pressed a few buttons on his phone. This action produced the sonically pleasing *beeps* and *bops* that activated his Projecto headband. It began to beam the just-predicted *wing zang zoom* montage, including some retro transitional wipes and dissolves in the shapes of hearts, teddy bears, and candy canes.

A mix of both video and still images of Katrina with Mr. Taffle showed them having the best time ever. The montage stopped on a picture of Katrina roller skating and licking her bubble-gum ice cream cone, while being pulled by a pack of Jack Russell puppies dressed as clowns. Mr. Taffle stared at the image. This was his favorite picture of the 'Katrina with Jack Russell Puppy Clowns' series, and a tear welled in his right eye.

"I still can't believe she was mine," whined Mr. Taffle out loud, as another tear now welled in his left eye. "I still can't believe how equally hot and cool she was. I still can't believe you can rent a gang of Jack Russell puppies dressed as clowns for any occasion. Kind of mind blowing, right?" He didn't answer himself.

Katrina's picture started to blink. This was the signal that someone was requesting to be projected out of the Projecto. Mr. Taffle pressed the flashing Mr. Manley's macho mustache icon, and Mr. Manley's projection appeared in front of him.

Mr. Manley held up and a spinning pinwheel, which made no sense unless one had read his heralded essay on "How Doing Things That Make No Sense Will Let You Get Away with Tons, aka H.D.T.T.M.N.S.W.LY.G.A.W.T." However, Mr. Taffle had not been privy to that essay. To qualify to read it one must first become a Big Champ and be granted the secret grip of the alpha dog handshake.

"I'll take Obsessing Over Your Way-Too-Hot-For-You Ex-Girlfriend for a hundred," announced Mr. Manley. He wore a game-show host smirk that looked exactly like his normal smirk.

"How do you know these things?" wondered a baffled Mr. Taffle.

"It's called critical thinking. If you utilized it, then you would know that your brain's not ready for that yet. But you *are* ready to hear an amazing story about the miracle of the human race known as Mr. Manley (aka me), and about the first time he banged the Big Gong. Now, Mr. Manley (aka me) originally thought that banging a gong to celebrate winning a sales award was very idiotic, and that's why he passionately loved the idea of it. So, there he was, about to bang the Big Gong and be crowned the Mighty Warlord. However, when he grabbed onto the gong mallet, he was suddenly overcome by a mystifyingly powerful sensation. He was being electrocuted. And then he died." Mr. Manley blew his pinwheel for 11 seconds before continuing.

"I'm once again lying. He didn't die. This feeling was THE *SIZZLE*! The point of this story is that..." Mr. Taffle waited silently for 11 more seconds. Then finally he continued, "...you don't have the *sizzle*, and Mr. Manley (aka me) DOES—nah nahny nah nah. And now, I'm afraid your future at Mr. Winkie's Electronics is at DEFCON .9997.6 And you know very well what will happen if the Top Doggies decide to round those numbers up."

Mr. Taffle couldn't believe what was happening. It seemed like just yesterday that he was *chomping* through the trainee program like an intern piranha, and now he was just one rounding-up away from the Top Doggies leaving him soaked in the gutter.

"What can I do to avoid the fire engine spray-down?!" pleaded Mr. Taffle.

"Mr. Taffle, I have the answer. But first, I need you to PayPal me $500 and then Venmo me $600."

How could Mr. Manley joke around at a time like this? thought Mr. Taffle. Somehow, Mr. Manley heard his thoughts and answered, "I'm not joking. And you've finally reached the bribing portion of your sales training. Congrats, Mr. Taffle. I owe you one donut hole of the computer's choosing. Okay, now I need you to focus with SOME DAMN PASSION!"

Mr. Taffle's eyebrow immediately elevated into Spock position. Not because he was just pretending to concentrate, but because he was so used to the Spock eyebrow-raise being his *I'm showing you how seriously I'm concentrating* look that it had actually become his real *I'm seriously concentrating*. This had been added onto the list of Taffle Tells.

Mr. Manley's projection traveled all the way back to the furthest part of the room, until he looked like he was the size of an Oreo cookie.

"Mr. Taffle, tonight you must go and get..." His projection rushed dramatically towards Mr. Taffle like an oncoming 3D locomotive. Mr. Manley was yelling, "...LOOOOOOSEY GOOOOOOOOSEY!"

Mr. Manley had perfectly timed the "Goosey" to end when he was just an inch away from Mr. Taffle's face. Mr. Manley then began to bite down continuously, like a guinea pig gnawing hungrily on a pellet.

"Okay, okay. I can get loosey goosey," said Mr. Taffle. However, he quickly descended into severe self-doubt. "If I knew exactly what you mean by that... because I don't."

"Well, the Loosey Goosey Report explains how this philosophy directly correlates with the *sizzle* and how they feed off each other like little fishes sucking microbes off a shark's naughty bits. Unfortunately, in order to be granted access to the Loosey Goosey file, you first have to read my essay "H.D.T.T.M.N.S.W.LY.G.A.W.T." Mr. Manley explained as if he were speaking to a 10-year-old with severe ADHD. "However," he continued, "I will overrule myself this one time and give you your first Loosey Goosey action step."

Mr. Taffle quickly grabbed a pen and notepad off the table to take notes and, of course, raised his right eyebrow into Spock position.

"You should start by swinging by Big Z's pad," began Mr. Manley. "You need to look him dead in the eye, man to man, and convince him to go forward with that deal. And if that doesn't work, then you can remind him of your mother's bag of tricks." Mr. Taffle concentrated hard on visions of piglets and panda bears twirling over pink marshmallow castles. "Oh, and I have Mr. Ziska's address, which I'm now texting to you. I'm surrounding it with emojis of smiling chickens and a woman's bonnet with a blue ribbon.

"You really think it's appropriate to just show up at Mr. Ziska's unannounced?" asked Mr. Taffle. He spoke in the same manner as Alex Trebek when he read the questions and answers on *Jeapordy*.

"It may not be appropriate, but it is LOOOOOOOSEY GOOOOOOSEY!" echoed Mr. Manley (he had put on a trippy echo effect called Trippy Echo). "LOOSEY GOOSEY, LOOSEY GOOSEY,

LOOSEY GOOSEY, LOOSEY GOOSEY, LOOSEY GOOSEY, LOOSEY GOOSEY...LOOSEY!" Mr. Manley's projection disappeared on the last "Loosey."

Mr. Taffle googled the definition for loosey goosey; the top definition was: NOT *following prescribed guideline or general societal expectations*. And that seemed right on the money. However, Mr. Taffle knew Mr. Manley's tendency for being diabolically crafty well. So, he most likely had a clever spin on this definition.

But now, knowing that his mother might be at Big Z's house when he made an unannounced visit, even if she was simply enjoying an innocent cup of coffee, made him feel more than a tad nauseous.

"I don't want to!" whined Mr. Taffle, and then knocked over the Keytar Clothing and Pipe Shop bag. This caused the pants to spill out onto the floor. He stared at the pants; he really did like them sooooooo much.

Strangely—it seemed as if the pants were staring back at him. Somehow, he felt positive that the pants wanted him to put them on soooooooo bad.

Mr. Taffle slipped on the pants. He had forgotten to put on underwear, but this wasn't that unusual. *That's odd*, Mr. Taffle thought, as he once again saw himself glow for a half a second. "And how badass do I look in these pants! I can't get over it!"

He suddenly felt compelled to unleash a series of sorry front karate kicks that made him stumble just like when he had been drunk for the only time in his life (turns out SVEDKA blue raspberry really wasn't soda pop from Sweden). In order to save face with the pants, he continued into a dive roll—which, to his amazement, he completed successfully—but then slammed straight into the wall. This left a bruise on his chest that made him look like he had a third nipple.

"Ouch," said Mr. Taffle.

Chapter Six
The Truth

Life can change on a dime. One minute you're watching *Jeopardy*, eating your sea bass dinner on your faux-fur saucer chair and sulking about your ex. And the next minute, you're speeding down the highway about to confront the president of one of the biggest financial corporations in the world. You're dressed in leather pants, casual black Hush Puppies, and a form-fitting black shirt that Katrina had once said made your muscles look bigger. You had worn that style shirt every single day since.

Mr. Taffle was surprised that he was headed downtown, so he said out loud, "I am surprised I am heading downtown." He realized then that he was actually talking to... his pants. Mr. Taffle had pictured Mr. Ziska living in a palatial estate somewhere up in the hills, surrounded by lush vegetation. His mother loved lush vegetation, and what did that matter?

The English woman from his Never Be Late app interrupted him, "Yeah, why wouldn't we be going downtown, since Mr. Ziska lives there—at least according to the address you gave me. And I have no reason to lie."

The English woman seemed insecure; this was perplexing on its own. But the fact that she had never been programmed to be the voice of his GPS really threw Mr. Taffle for a loop. Not to mention, the voice had the minor slur of someone who might have thrown down more than a few too many pints at the pub while pretending to enjoy watching cricket on the telly. What the hell was going on? Had his GPS gone rogue on him? He laughed out loud, tickled at the idea.

And then the English woman laughed along with him. It was the kind of laugh that was usually meant for kissing ass. He knew this because it sounded exactly like his own laugh when comunicating with everyone. But this laugh could also indicate that one might be hiding something, as Mr. Manley had once pointed out while dangling Mr. Taffle above the fifth-floor garbage chute, determined to find out what he was hiding.

What in the hell was he thinking?! He needed to get out of his head and focus on saving the deal, as well as what he might say to his mother if she answered the door in her pajamas.

The buildings started to get taller at the same rate as the streets got narrower and the streetlights got dimmer. It was actually a pretty neat effect that Mr. Taffle might have enjoyed if he hadn't been petrified about driving at night, especially on a work/school night. As an excuse not to go out anywhere, Mr. Taffle would often pretend that his TV was his pet and that it would get lonely if he were gone after dark. He would pet the screen and fully extend the retractable neck of the flat screen wall mount to give the illusion that the TV had a neck. He secretly named the TV "Neeneer."

"Take a left at Reddu Road," said the English woman, giving only two seconds of warning before they came to the intersection. Mr. Taffle slammed on the brakes and barely made the turn, leaving skid marks on the road. Whoa! He had never done that before.

"I'm not used to giving directions," apologized the English woman, as her voice climbed an unnatural octave higher. "Also, take a left at Reddu Avenue *now!*" Mr. Taffle went hard into the turn at the widest possible arc and drove on the sidewalk for a quick moment. "So sorry. I'm doing the best I can, and that's all you can do in the end. Go left at Reddu Way RIGHT NOW!!!"

Mr. Taffle fishtailed into an alley, miraculously donuting into the one empty parking spot in a lot of six spaces. This amazing stunt had been performed in four of Burt Reynolds' films made between 1979 and 1983.

Burt Reynolds had been ranked *the 7th greatest former macho mustache man with a top-rated man perm,* according to Mr. Manley's spreadsheet.

"You have arrived," announced the voice of Morgan Freeman, who was the voice Mr. Taffle had actually programmed into his GPS. But Mr. Taffle didn't pay attention to Morgan Freeman. This might have seemed disrespectful, if not for the fact that directly in front of him there had appeared a jaw-dropping, blinking, 50-foot white neon-light question mark mounted on a 51-foot brick wall.

This can't be where Mr. Ziska lives, he thought. There's no way in the world he could ever have imagined his mother coming to this part of town, and why should she?

Mr. Taffle approached the wall, looking for an address, when an unseen male voice whispered to him all *Lord of the Rings*y meets *Harry Pottery*, "Do you seek The Truth?"

Mr. Taffle jumped back. "Who said that?" Mr. Taffle looked in every possible direction. "Mr. Ziska. Is that you?"

"Sorry, that's not the password."

"Who's talking?"

"I'm talking."

"Who are you?"

"I'm The Wall."

And then a man in full body paint camouflage appeared as if magically coming out of the wall. Half of The Wall's body was painted like the bricks, and the other half was painted to perfectly match where it turned to shadow.

"That's really outstanding body paint," marveled Mr. Taffle.

"It's the very best body paint on the market, so I'd hope so," said The Wall in an automatic response reserved for everyone.

"I must be at the wrong address. Sorry to bother you," Mr. Taffle said with an apologetic smile. As Mr. Taffle turned around, the luminosity of the question mark perfectly illuminated his pants.

"Hey, I really love your pants," said The Wall. "Where did you get them?"

This was the second-best compliment Mr. Taffle had ever received. The first had been when Katrina admitted to him, "I have an extreme nerd fetish, so you're like a dreamboat to me."

"I bought them today at The Keytar Clothing and Pipe Shop."

"I didn't ask you when you bought them, but thanks for sharing that. Well, I guess you can go into The Truth without the password."

"Go in where?"

"Are you serious? I just told you!" snapped The Wall.

Mr. Taffle had no idea what to say next. He had meant his question literally: Where should I enter? There was no door to be seen. Not to mention that he was extremely wary of starting some nightmare Abbot and Costello *Who's on First* skit comedy black hole.

"The bar's name is The Truth, okay? Got it? 'Cause if I have to tell you again, I'm going to finally quit this damn job." The Wall would never quit his dream job, but he wanted to let Mr. Taffle know he wasn't messing around. "Now, dig this..."

The Wall flirtatiously winked, although you couldn't see him wink; his eyeballs were also realistically painted as bricks. The Wall reached behind his back and pulled out a remote control. He punched a few buttons, and the entire question mark slid dramatically inward, revealing a pitch-black passageway.

"Enter... quickly... before I get busted for letting you in without the password."

No way in hell was Mr. Taffle entering into this question-mark dungeon. Besides, he couldn't lose his focus; he still needed to confront Mr. Ziska and save the deal. However, suddenly Mr. Taffle's right leg lunged forward.

"I didn't do that... did I?" thought Mr. Taffle. And then both of his legs went gently rogue on him. His legs marched forward gingerly. He felt like a scrawny marching band tuba player who could barely support the weight of the tuba, and his face revealed the same look that one would get the moment they realized they had voluntarily chosen to play the tuba. The Wall stared deeply at Mr. Taffle's pants, as the question mark closed behind him.

Mr. Taffle could feel a throbbing bass in his bones as he walked ahead through the pitch-dark tunnel. This throbbing bass wasn't by coincidence; it had been specifically designed to lead someone through the darkness and to increase their anticipation of what was coming. The pitch for this special entrance had been titled,

"The Throbbing Bass Tunnel of Mystery and Intrigue." And while it did work pretty much like the original bullet point presentation promised it would, it really was just the tip of the iceberg.

"Because when you enter a seven-story nightclub that's a stylistic tribute to Dutch graphic artist M.C. Escher's "Relativity", while militantly continuing with the question-mark theme, you're doing okay," said one of The Truth's bartenders. He had said this to at least one customer every night since he'd started working there a year ago.

Here were some of the highlights: The rows of bar stools appeared to run horizontally, but as one approached, the optical illusion was dispelled, revealing that the rows were actually vertical. There were real reflections of fake reflections and staircases on the ceiling leading into realistic sketches of hallways. And, of course, question marks of every shape and size appeared everywhere.

The owners had come up with an innovative way to form a class system within the walls of the club without needing to create a VIP section. This was the main reason The Truth had been approved to be the cornerstone nightclub in the *secret* part of the city. The head of the City Council—who remained anonymous, but everyone called her the Duchess—had been a big fan of this concept.

Getting the Duchess' approval was all one needed, as the City Council was just a front for her to appear as if she cared about anyone's opinion but her own. This would become common knowledge once it was too late to back out.

In order to claim VIP status at The Truth, one had to follow a strict dress code. The code was an homage to the 1980s new wave band A Flock of Seagulls. Surprisingly, the dress code was not based on the band's famous hairstyle, which resembled the wings of a bird in flight on either side of the head, with a downward-facing swoop in the middle that covered one eye. (This hairstyle had required using a concoction of mousse, gel, hairspray, and a souped-up, high-powered blow dryer.)

Instead, The Truth's entire VIP dress code was based on the two femme fatales who catwalked across the stage in the "I Ran" hit music video while the pasty-white new wave band members spun around in a room of mirrors and smoke machines. The femme fatales' outfits consisted of black vinyl onesies with red satin obi-like sashes; shiny, thigh-high black stiletto boots; and sharp, pointy shoulder pads. This look coordinated perfectly with their red-and-black raccoon face paint and red faux hawks.

In accordance with the exciting new *Sexism is Bad* policy, it had been decided that male patrons would also be required to dress in the femme fatale style in order to qualify for VIP status. A groundbreaking scanner had been invented for The Truth, its sole purpose being to determine just how closely each patron's outfit, makeup, and hairstyle resembled those of the femme fatales. This measurement would determine how long each patron would wait in line for a drink. It would also determine the level of ass-kissing each patron would receive from the bartender.

Mr. Taffle made his way through the crowded bar. It was filled with 642 of the retro-futuristic femme fatales, as well as 23 patrons not participating in the VIP dress code system. The majority of drinkers sipped brightly colored drinks from laser gun-shaped martini glasses. The "guns" would randomly shoot violet and dark orange laser beams across the room.

Mr. Taffle took note that everyone in the bar looked as if they were in on some big secret that he was not privy to. The mysterious, foreboding expression they wore was a similar to the look the femme fatales had worn in the video. Mastering this mysterious look got every VIP 20% off the drinks served in the martini laser guns.

Mr. Taffle continued up a winding staircase to a third-level bar. In reality, it was actually a reflection of the bar coming from the fourth level. So he walked all the way down the winding staircase and up a neighboring jagged staircase whose every fifth step featured a flashing strobe light.

Once Mr. Taffle made it up to the fourth level, he realized that the refection had just been a drawing of the bar... which he now saw was really located in the southwest corner of a room on the sixth level.

"What the heck!" he squealed, as a searchlight from the roof revealed a hidden horizontal set of stairs that ran along the wall.

"Sweetness."

As Mr. Taffle carefully traversed this narrow secret staircase, he noticed that there was a glass cage hanging high above on the roof. Inside the cage was an alpaca wearing a custom-made disco ball suit. The outfit included cute disco ball earmuffs and cute disco ball slippers. Every five minutes, the alpaca's cage was illuminated by bolts of electricity that sent cute cartoon electric alpaca reflections flooding down over the entire bar.

The last person to have seen this effect happen for the first time had said, "This somehow knocks the trippiness level up a notch and a half, and I didn't think that was possible. Although it really doesn't the match the theme, I'm not complaining; I'm just stating the obvious."

Mr. Taffle grabbed the last available bar stool in the middle of the vertical bar. The bar itself ran up the wall until it disappeared into a giant black mirror. Mr. Taffle buckled himself in with a bar stool seatbelt, which held him in surprising comfort at a 45° angle. He confidently motioned to the bartender for a drink. The bartender, instead of wearing femme fatale attire, was dressed as The Flock of Seagulls' lead singer (with the aforementioned haircut). But, even though he looked directly at Mr. Taffle, he walked right past him.

Mr. Taffle was used to this ho-hum blow-off routine. He had experienced it his entire life, excluding the *miracles really do happen if you just believe you can fly then you can really touch the sky* stretch when he was dating Katrina. However, then the bartender accidentally caught a glimpse of Mr. Taffle's pants in the reflection of the mirror behind the bar. Seeing them, he immediately pivoted back, totally ignoring the VIP outfit-scanner alarm beeping annoyingly at him to ignore this non-VIP.

"What can I get for you, sir?" asked the bartender.

"I'll have a Fuzzy Navy," answered Mr. Taffle, surprising himself with the coolness that he had practiced for months while ordering this specific drink for the open-bar portion of the Mighty Warlord Extravaganza.

The bartender knew that Mr. Taffle had really meant to order a Fuzzy Navel. That mistake would technically give the bartender clearance by the computer to be a snotty jerk. This was a job perk the bartender had never passed up. But then he got another look at Mr. Taffle's pants and shockingly felt like being helpful, for reasons that didn't revolve around getting tips or sex.

"You meant Fuzzy Navel, right?" the bartender whispered tenderly.

"Oh, my gosh. I can't believe I said Fuzzy Navy. I really, really do suck," sighed Mr. Taffle. But this refreshingly nice bartender just smiled like a refreshingly nice guy.

"No, you don't. It happens all the time, sir. And may I suggest a fresh mint garnish on that Fuzzy Navel."

"That would be wonderful. Thank you so much..."

As the bartender walked away, a man with an unnaturally massive reddish nose sitting to his left spilled the umbrella pick of his tropical Mai Tai onto Mr. Taffle's left pant leg.

"I'm so sorry!" exclaimed the man. He grabbed his one cocktail napkin and desperately patted down Mr. Taffle's pant leg, even though barely any liquid had spilled.

"That's okay. Accidents happen all the time. Trust me, I'm an expert." Mr. Taffle smiled in the same nice-guy way the bartender had just smiled at him, and he instantaneously felt positive about contributing to spreading the love.

"I had a feeling you were an expert, so double thanks for not punching me in my nose. I just got another nose job this week," said the man as he inadvertently broke the umbrella pick into pieces on Mr. Taffle's leg. He continued to clean the pants as if he were shining shoes.

This unnecessary cleaning would have seemed really strange if Mr. Taffle hadn't been so hung up on the question: "This man had a nose job?!" His nose was maybe the biggest he'd ever seen. A nose *extension* maybe? Was that a thing?

Then Mr. Taffle noticed something else odd about the man: He was dressed in a trash bag. However, upon further examination, it became clear that this was actually the same getup everyone else was wearing in The Truth—just the cheapest version possible. The trash bag was in place of the femme fatale black vinyl onesie, and instead of the red satin obi, it was tied together with a pinkish dyed cotton twine rope.

The man also wore some children's football shoulder pads that he had found at his daily hangout—the dumpster behind Jamba Juice. Only his boots were off-theme; they were the demon monster boots that Gene Simmons (from the rock band KISS) had popularized. The man had stolen them from a Gene Simmons tribute artist, who he always bragged was the second-best tribute artist he'd seen. ("The Rod Stewart lookalike in Reno will forever be the Holy Grail!")

Amazingly, the VIP outfit scanner hadn't taken off points for the KISS boots. "I was admiring your totally bitching leather pants, and I think I got a tad envious. That made my cocktail wrist go limp for a brief moment. It's really embarrassing when that happens."

"Again, it's not a big deal…"

"You see, I was going to buy a pair just like those. But I ended up buying some cheaper imitation leather pants with randomly placed zippers that run across and down the legs. I was crazy to think they were going to compensate for the real thing," he chuckled.

"Well, you should go out and treat yourself to a real pair of leather pants, if that's how you feel," encouraged Mr. Taffle, who again felt the love by spreading the love.

"I know I should. I just don't quite have the wallet for that right now," the man admitted.

Mr. Taffle's mouth promptly watered until a thick puddle of drool collected under his tongue. Oh snap! Did Pavlov's dog just bark at the Pleebley Weebly's front door? As the bartender dropped off the Fuzzy Navel, Mr. Taffle made the split-second decision to take out a $20 bill and leave it as a tip for the bartender.

Mr. Taffle casually glanced at the other man's throat and watched him gulp down a thick puddle of his own drool at the sight of his baller tip. Holy moley! It worked! The Pleebley Weebly Pavlov's Dog Drool Transfer was a technique Mr. Manley had demonstrated to him in the port-a-john at their Meet Your Mentor Q & A Picnic by using animatics with a temp score from the overture of the *Jesus Christ Superstar* soundtrack. Now, if this man introduced himself in the next five seconds, then it would officially be a Pleebley Weebly Bum Rush.

"My name is Jackson, but most people call me Jack Honey Badger. I think it's because there's a few gals who think I'm kind of sweet," gushed Jack Honey Badger.

Mr. Taffle had watched a series of viral videos that showcased just how crazy and dangerous the actual honey badger is. The videos were narrated by a guy with an Australian accent, which helped drive home the zany aggressiveness of the honey badger in the same way a Morgan Freeman voiceover invokes heartwarming feelings of an oncoming mystical roller-coaster ride with global implications. This was the reason Mr. Taffle had selected the "Morgan Freeman" voice option for his GPS in the first place.

Maybe his nickname is a red flag? Nah. Don't talk yourself out of turning off the nuclear vacuum mid-Pleebley Weebly suck-a-thon, he thought. He continued.

"You know, it wasn't too long ago Jack Honey Badger, that my wallet wouldn't let me buy a pair of leather pants either. But I've worked pretty hard for the last year, and it's really paying off. I just put a down payment on my first jet ski. I've always wanted one, so that was pretty sweet."

"Oh, my God! I've always told anyone who would listen that one day I would own my own jet ski!" shouted a stoked Jack Honey Badger.

"Cool, cool, cool. Well, I haven't even properly introduced myself. My name is Mr. Taffle. I work for Mr. Winkie's Electronics, and we don't believe in using first names," he said, going into the Spock eyebrow raise for no apparent reason.

"Look, I usually don't talk business when I'm out at the hottest nightclubs, but I've got a feeling that you would be an ideal candidate to join the Mr. Winkie's sales team. We're creating a sales army to invade not just the world, but also all of the most popular virtual universes in the trendiest metaverses. And all because of this baby..." Mr. Taffle bit his tongue as panic shot through his body. Had he forgotten to bring a Projecto headband with him?

He reached nervously down to check both of his pant pockets simultaneously. Whew! Mr. Taffle hadn't brought just one Projecto in his left pocket as usual, but he'd also put an extra one in his right pocket, and one more extra in his back pocket. So strange that he couldn't remember doing that.

"I'm going to give you something, Jack Honey Badger, but I want you to promise not to open it until we talk on the phone in a few days."

"I know we just met, but I'm the type of guy you can count on to keep his promise," vowed Jack Honey Badger earnestly.

Mr. Taffle took one of the Projecto headband cases out of his pocket and slid it across the bar to Jack Honey Badger. Each headband case had been designed to look like a safe from a bank vault. This design brought up the cost of manufacturing the Projecto significantly but was approved by Mr. Winkie because they looked "tough". Mr. Taffle then mimed the words "I'm so intrigued" at the same time Jack Honey Badger did, making it official. Mr. Manley was right when he said he was always right.

"Wait till you hear about the life discou-n-t..."

Mr. Taffle had brought up the damn life discount! Once again, he was going to burn the Pleebley Weebly Toast, and no amount of Pleebley Weelby Miracle Whip was going to make that sweet again.

"Life discount?!" rejoined Jack Honey Badger. "I'm sorry, Mr. Taffle, but it's just hard to believe that I'm really going to get a life discount. You're a real good dude, and I appreciate it."

Mr. Taffle couldn't help but take a victorious spin in the barstool, which took a lot of effort, as it was, again, on a 45° angle.

As he came full circle, he felt his fragile heart dip completely into his sulfuric acid-filled soul. No, this wasn't from the fast spin, but because of what he had just seen. No way! It couldn't be: Sitting in a corner booth was someone who looked exactly like KAAATRRRIIIINAAAAHHHHH.

He took another spin to get a better look. This time, he was joined by Jack Honey Badger, who only made it halfway around, as he hadn't properly estimated the effort needed for a 360° spin at a 45° angle. It had to be Katrina! Even if it wasn't Katrina, he still had to meet this woman; she looked even hotter! Mr. Taffle felt immediately ashamed for being honest with himself. As for Katrina, she was dressed in a sparkling disco ball unitard, sitting next to an exact lookalike mannequin dressed in an identical unitard. These outfits were suspiciously similar to the one worn by the Disco Ball Alpaca hanging above.

"I've got to go," muttered Mr. Taffle.

"Okay, I'm okay with that, okay," Jack Honey Badger stated calmly, "despite the rowdy collision of man's primal urges that just unleashed the lust of modern technological luxuries straight into my superego. So maybe do a brother a solid and divulge the life discount before you split." Mr. Taffle heard exactly zero words just said. Jack Honey Badger was not surprised at being tuned out, because this had happened to him every day since he had learned how to speak. But he always continued to talk anyway, as he found that this was his best chance for someone to accidentally listen. "Well, perhaps I should tell you about how swollen my fist is going to be after it repeatedly punches you in the nose. I'll probably have to go to some specialist for months because of how messed up my fist is going to be from punching you repeatedly in the nose. In fact, when it's all said and done, my fist will probably be much worse than your nose. And you're not going to even have a nose anymore. You're going to be noseless. What happened to my nose? I can't smell anything. How did I get here?"

For no apparent reason, the only words Mr. Taffle heard were *swollen* and *specialist*.

"Have my Fuzzy Navy," mumbled Mr. Taffle as he slid his drink to Jack Honey Badger, unbuckled his stool's seat belt, and stumbled away.

CHAPTER SEVEN

Mannequins And Heartbreaks

Mr. Taffle descended a steep staircase that zigzagged down the wall, not even noticing the crisscross of laser fire shooting around him from random femme fatales' martini-glass stems. He was zeroed in on Katrina. What in the world would he say to her? How have you been? Where did you move? Why did you ghost me on such a diabolical level?

As Mr. Taffle approached the corner booth, he locked eyes with... Katrina's mannequin. As Mr. Taffle looked deep into the mannequin's mouthwash-blue eyes, all the negativity he had held in—from having had his heart pulverized—dissolved like the cotton candy he had shared with Katrina at the Cirque du Soleil. He'd sold his plasma for six weeks straight in order to raise funds for their baller third-row tickets. He was honestly happy just to see Katrina, even if just in the form of a duplicate bald mannequin.

He finally broke free of the mannequin's intoxicating gaze and turned his head to face the real Katrina. "Hey, didn't we go out once?" joked Mr. Taffle as he pinched his left nipple, which was now on the list of The Taffle Tells, as this happened every time he was nervous or said something cheesy.

Katrina looked up, trying to process that Mr. Taffle was indeed in right front of her. "You're here... in front of me... wearing leather pants. What? How?"

If someone didn't know better, her halting speech could have caused them to mistake her for a malfunctioning super-sexy cyborg that was clearly ripping off Jane Fonda in Barbarella.

"Well, Katrina, actually—"

Katrina quickly leaned forward, bringing her mannequin with her. "You can't call me Katrina in here. Please, call me The Mannequin Madam," she whispered, as if talking to both Mr. Taffle and the mannequin. "Now, please, laugh as if I just told you a semi-funny joke."

"Okay," responded Mr. Taffle in a measured nervous chuckle that nobody would buy as genuine laughter.

"Actually, please don't call me by my first name either. Just call me Mr. Taffle. That's not me just trying to one-up your alias game; the company I work for gives me points if you participate in a survey asking you if I told you my first name. I know how weird that sounds... and why am I telling you all this? I'm sorry, I'm just nervous. This is just such a crazy coincidence running into you."

"It is quite a coinkadink... Mr. Taffle. And this is Monique the Mannequin."

Mr. Taffle playfully waved at Monique and then affectionately rubbed her bald head.

"Please don't do that. She doesn't like that."

"Okay. Sorry," he said with a half-smile.

"I know, I must seem totally cuckoo for Cocoa Puffs," she said returning the half-smile.

This self-deprecating analogy—comparing her mental state to a sugar cereal—reassured Mr. Taffle that Katrina was probably mentally okay... and how did she get even hotter? It was seriously weird.

"I'm aware of what a talented artist you are. You know how much I adored your smoky man ceramic incense holders. Are you still making them?" he asked.

"No, I haven't done anything very artistic for a while. I've been getting more into acting, actually. But I really need to get back into it."

"Well, I think that calling yourself The Mannequin Madam and carrying around your own duplicate mannequin is next-level performance art. It's a fresh of breath air."

"That's very sweet of you," she said. As she was finishing her sentence, she decided not to mention his accidental word scramble.

"So, are you still selling the coupon calendars?"

"No, I quit that a while ago. I think I lost my passion for it maybe because, well... you were the coupon calendar model, and it got a tad awkward when, every time I had to open the calendar in front of a perspective client, I would fall to the ground in a panic attack. I'm kidding... sort of."

"Do you mind if we don't talk about the past quite yet?"

"No, no... NO!" he thought. Mr. Taffle wanted to talk about it! But, as it turned out, despite their time apart, he would still do whatever she commanded.

"Okay, no talk about the past... for now."

"Thank you, Mr. Taffle," she said.

"You're welcome," he said. They had a history of always being very polite with each other.

"Actually, leaving the coupon calendar industry was the best thing that ever happened to me, professionally speaking. I now work in the sales department of Mr. Winkie's Electronics."

"This is the same company that has the survey I take to inform them that you didn't reveal your first name to me?"

"I know that Mr. Winkie's unorthodox sales techniques do sound ridiculous when you say them out loud. But, amazingly, they work like magic," he said, realizing that they still sounded ridiculous. "Okay, so, now you must think that I'm the one who's cuckoo for the Cocoa Puffs."

"Oh, absolutely," she giggled. It was that same giggle that Mr. Taffle heard in his head over and over whenever he played the *wing zang zoom* montage from his Projecto while bawling profusely.

"I can actually show you the product I'm selling, if you have your phone on you?" The Mannequin Madam leaned over and pretended Monique whispered in her ear.

"Looks like Monique saved the day again!" she cheered as she reached into Monique's front hidden pouch and pulled out her phone.

"Is my number still programmed into your phone?" he asked, as he dug his fingernails into his palms.

"No," she casually replied.

Mr. Taffle realized right then that life was indeed just a brutal pain machine with rechargeable batteries. He silently vowed to himself to leave everything behind. He would start smoking hashish, travel around with no shoes, and preach out of a bullhorn the truth about how love is really just a chemical in the brain. Love is an illusion. It's not real, brother!

"Of course, I still have your digits," said The Mannequin Madam with a playful wink. And in the blink of an eye, Mr. Taffle's entire future yo-yoed back and forth. Wheeeeew.

"I'm now going to trade you your phone for one of these headbands with a mini-camera on it."

"Okay, you've got me curious."

"You ain't seen nothing yet," he playfully teased.

This was the same teasing charm that Mr. Taffle had originally laid on thick when they had first met at the coupon calendar shoot for the month of November. He had volunteered to let the turkey in the Thanksgiving-themed monthly shoot peck away at his face between camera setups in order to *let the turkey get it out of its system.* Mr. Taffle had kept joking about how Katrina was really missing out, as the bird stabbed its beak through his upper lip, requiring him to receive eight stitches. Katrina had felt sorry for him, which was the thing that ignited the first spark. So it had been totally worth the intense pain.

"Okay, now, face the opposite direction, and when I ring you, I just need you to do one thing..." Mr. Taffle milked this for a long beat. "Answer."

The Mannequin Madam's phone rang on cue. It was the same *mysterious suspense* ringtone he had programmed into his phone. In any normal situation, this would be noted as an amazing coincidence.

"KILLER DILLER!" she applauded as both of their projections appeared out of their Projecto headbands.

"Welcome to Projecto! And it even comes with Feel Technology. So, if you want to slap me in the face, you can," said Mr. Taffle, bracing to get slapped as usual.

"I would never slap you... unless that's what you *wanted*," she purred.

"Thank you."

"You're welcome. And I'm so happy for you. What an exciting product to be selling."

"Thank you."

"You're welcome. And I love your new look with the leather pants."

"Thank you. Honestly, this is the first time I've ever worn leather pants. I actually bought them to wear to my company's yearly award ceremony tomorrow, if you can believe that."

"Haven't you heard the golden rule that you should never mix business with leather?" The Mannequin Madam's projection chuckled, and Mr. Taffle's projection smiled. It was clear that these two had an amazing chemistry, despite their major gap in hotness.

"So, what are you doing here anyway?" asked Mr. Taffle.

"Hey, did you know there's a secret level in this place that contains a museum of swords called... The Museum of Swords?" she quickly interjected, as if she didn't hear the question. Mr. Taffle knew she was trying to change the subject, but he was going to let it slide; she had officially assumed control of him again.

"No way. A museum, at a bar? Maybe this is my kind of joint after all."

"I know how passionate you are about memorizing fun facts; that's why I mentioned it. It's quite an impressive collection, and you'll learn a lot about swords and how they played a vital role in world history. Although, I must admit, it's almost impossible to find the invisible door that leads you up to a staircase and then into the floor where it's located."

"This place is just so bonkers," reflected Mr. Taffle with a facial gesture he thought made him look bonkers. Instead, he just appeared to have a severe learning disability. This would have come across as offensive if Katrina didn't know what a good dude he was. "It's like a question mark-themed maze, with secret hallways that are really just fake reflections coming from another side of the room that's on another level—and my brain is going to explode."

"You ain't seen nothing yet," said The Mannequin Madam. "Once you enter through the wall, the only thing that will seem strange is when something is normal. There's a rumor that this part of downtown was created by a radical experimental artist using alien technology with unlimited funds."

"I love that."

"And the truth is that The Truth is the perfect place to hide." She immediately regretted saying something so obviously revealing.

"Are you hiding from someone?" he casually asked, trying to keep his cool.

"I can't tell you. I don't want to put you in danger."

She *was* in danger! "You need to tell me so I can help you," demanded Mr. Taffle.

"You ask the question after he has already given you the answer."

"What?"

"He's never on your mind, but you're always on his mind."

"I have no idea what you're talking about."

"How could you? I'm not making any sense because I'm just a Tiddly Wink in his game of Tiddly Winks. That's all I can tell you."

"Well, I'm not leaving you until I know you're safe."

"Oh, Mr. Taffle, you're just the cat's meow. And I would really appreciate that."

"I know you don't want to talk about the past right now, but... the cat's meow is what you called me when..."

"...you first tried to kiss me," she said, finishing his sentence.

"Tried? Succeeded!" stated Mr. Taffle confidently. And then... smooch! The Mannequin Madam went in for a make-out session with Mr. Taffle's projection. Monique the Mannequin watched in silence.

"I swear I can feel your lips," The Mannequin Madam said, amazed.

"That's actually the Feel Technology," he said proudly. Then he realized that the happiest moment he'd had since the last time they'd kissed was about to be interrupted by a sudden and imperative need to pee.

"I'm so sorry, but I need to excuse myself," he blurted out, quickly standing up.

"Okay... but hurry back, Mr. Taffle," she said, sounding disappointed. He was unsure whether she was disappointed because he prematurely cut off the kiss or because someone was looking for her with bad intentions and she was afraid to be alone—not counting Monique, of course.

CHAPTER EIGHT

Oh Dear Lord

M r. Taffle traversed, crisscrossed, and descended seven different staircases until he finally found the one that led to the men's room. He sprinted right past The Bathroom Attendant, who was dressed in a 1930s zoot suit with a derby hat and was painted head to toe in bright white paint, which made him resemble a statue. There was a question mark painted on his forehead, as if this was his third eye. He used the same top-of-the-line body paint that The Wall had used, and this wasn't by coincidence. The Wall and The Bathroom Attendant had previously worked together at the Walken's Watch Gastropub (another themed bar in this secret part of the city). That bar had taken its theme from Christopher Walken's *Pulp Fiction* monologue involving a watch hidden up his character's butt.

However, while The Wall was given all the perks of a full-time employee, The Bathroom Attendant was still only an independent contractor and had to pay for his body paint himself. The Wall and The Bathroom Attendant had a history of not getting along. The Wall was so militantly by-the-book about everything that The Bathroom Attendant had called him Nazi Wall Boy behind his back on several occasions. Then one day a Viet Cong cocktail waitress finally ratted him out. This caused enough tension between the two that they almost had a dust-up at the company holiday party.

Mr. Taffle relieved himself as quickly as possible while still maintaining a controlled stream. At least he didn't suck at that. He then hurried to the sink, quickly washed his hands, and splashed water onto his face.

"*Sizzle, Sizzle, Sizzle,*" he hissed to his own reflection, in attempt to psych himself up for round two with The Mannequin Madam. But he realized that he had been in such a rush to pee that he hadn't even bothered to scope out the rest of the bathroom.

"The bathroom really is the crown jewel of the trippiness," said the guy who had just used the same exact latrine. As Mr. Taffle gazed around, he saw that the toilet stalls appeared to stretch on to infinity, as did the framed question-mark paintings and potted question-mark Chia Pets that lined the wall.

"Wow, that looks so real," marveled Mr. Taffle. Then he asked himself, "And why is there someone right behind me?" He glanced over his shoulder to find that The Bathroom Attendant was standing uncomfortably close to him, holding out a saucer full of mints in the shape of question marks.

"Hey, do you mind giving me the password so I can give you your question-mark mint and I can go on my break?" asked The Bathroom Attendant politely.

"Um, I actually don't know the password. The Wall let me in without it."

The Bathroom Attendant laughed so hard it turned into a coughing fit, which caused him to spill a few question-mark mints off the tray. "The Wall giving an inch to anyone about anything?" he thought. That was the biggest steaming pile of bull crap he'd ever heard. However, he had to remain somewhat professional, as he'd already been written up several times for being *dickish* to customers. Plus, he remembered that he loved this man's pants so much that everything had to work out. "Well, you're the customer, and theoretically the customer is always right. That being said, I'm still going on my break. Good luck," he said as he walked out.

Mr. Taffle doused his face with one more splash of water, gave another round of *sizzle* hisses to his reflection, and then turned around to leave.

"What happened to the door I came in?" he said to himself. The entire wall was now tiled as if the entrance had never existed.

"Huh? Huh? What? What?" Mr. Taffle walked up to the wall to investigate further. He searched for some kind of lever or button. He looked under the question mark trash can, under the question mark coat rack, and under all the question mark sinks. Nothing! He had to figure out a way to get back to The Mannequin Madam, as she had specifically requested he was to hurry. He preferred to obey her at all costs.

It took Mr. Taffle seven minutes and 41 seconds to sprint down the row of infinite toilet stalls, all the while looking for another exit. He had to take two quick breathers on the way, as well as a brief stretch as his calf muscles tightened. Finally, he saw that the 589th stall door had a flickering light coming from inside of it.

The light peeping out of the door was so intense that it seemed powerfully spiritual. This feeling was enhanced by the sound of sitars and hand drums coming from the next stall over. There was no toilet in this stall, only a giant question mark painted on the back wall.

As he fought through the intense glare of the light, he could see that the period on the question mark was actually a hole just big enough for Mr. Taffle to fit in. "Sizzle, Sizzle, Sizzle," hissed Mr. Taffle as he climbed into the question mark, and... ZOOOOOOOOOOM!

Like an inter-office package whooshing through one of those old-time pneumatic tubes, Mr. Taffle was whisked down the chute. As he was blasted out, he plunged down 50 feet onto a trampoline marked with a giant question mark.

He bounced back up another 20 feet, perfectly aimed into another hollow question mark tunnel. Next, he shot down a slide covered with the same chemical compound used to lube aircraft carrier engines. This made him slide almost three times faster than the world's fastest bobsled (its speed was 93 miles per hour—a fun fact that Mr. Taffle had memorized).

He was spit out perfectly onto a merry-go-round, mid-spin. The classic carousel horses had been replaced by horse-sized question marks, which were also rideable. *Once again, The Truth's consistent and brilliant thematic features were off the charts,* he somehow had time to think. He was surprised that he'd been able to keep his balance, but he knew deep down that this had been because of the pants.

As he spun around the merry-go-round, he could see that there were four different question mark tunnel exits. This roundabout design had been modeled after the most modern European roundabout roadways. An intern named Francine Carpenter had obtained the detailed schematics of the roundabouts off the Internet for free. It had been considered quite a score at the time. In fact, this discovery had gotten her promoted to the position of Second Assistant to the VP of Research for The Truth.

All four of the question marks exits were exactly the same, but Mr. Taffle somehow knew his pants wanted to exit via the fourth question mark tunnel. He spun off the merry-go-round into the tunnel... and slammed straight into Jack Honey Badger, who happened to be waiting there. It was as if he had somehow known Mr. Taffle was coming, and this disturbed Mr. Taffle even more than had the over-the-top chaotic ride. Both men toppled violently onto the ground.

"Oh, hey, Mr. Taffle." Jack Honey Badger casually greeted him with a little wave. "You running straight into me again: What a cowinkydink! And I'm not just saying cowinkydink because I... didn't hear the woman with the mannequin say that to you when... I wasn't spying on you," he rambled, as they both slowly rose to their feet.

Annoyed, Mr. Taffle said, "Look, I told you that I would call you in a few days pal, so please relax."

"Oh, I'm chillaxing very hard right now, thank you," responded Jack Honey Badger. "But you didn't even say goodbye. And that's no way to treat an ideal candidate!"

"Well, don't worry about it, because you're no longer an ideal candidate, okay? Now, I've got to go, sir!" Mr. Taffle was surprised he had raised his voice, as he had always tried to live by the mantra, "Avoid getting punched in the face at all costs."

"So, you're rescinding my ideal-candidate status? Is there any possible way you will reconsider your decision?" calmly asked Jack Honey Badger.

"No chance," said Mr. Taffle. At that, Jack Honey Badger immediately sprinted out of the room at top speed.

Well, if that wasn't the weirdest bathroom story in the history of people going to the bathroom, Mr. Taffle reflected. *And I guess it's going to get still weirder,* he thought, as Jack Honey Badger returned, holding two ancient swords.

"I have a 15th-century replica Swiss longsword in my left hand and a 14th-century replica Japanese katana in my right hand. Choose your sword wisely!" he said while swinging both swords in a circle as if he were jumping rope.

"What do you think is going to happen here? You think we're going to sword fight?"

"Oh, you want to sword fight?! I accept! Well, I'm picking the Swiss sword, since they're also ground zero for hot cocoa and they hold the ancient secrets of the fondue. Now, prepare to die by a neutral sword!"

Jack Honey Badger tossed Mr. Taffle the katana carefully, making it easy to catch.

"We're not going to—" Before Mr. Taffle could finish, Jack Honey Badger charged with his sword, swinging it like a fly swatter in a swarm of flies.

Mr. Taffle barely blocked the windmill blade with his sword. This caused Mr. Taffle's sword to deflect off Jack Honey Badger's blade, which then ricocheted upwards and cut off Jack Honey Badger's nose. His nose bounced down the tunnel like a golf ball on concrete. Both men screamed simultaneously. Jack Honey Badger screamed from the horror of having the fake rubber nose being sliced off his face for the second time in a week. Mr. Taffle screamed at the realization that Jack Honey Badger didn't have a nose at all. It was just two holes on a bump that looked like the snout of... a beaver? An otter? A wolverine?

"So, I guess now the badger is out of the bag. Yes, I'm that lad who had his nose punched so many times that he lost his nose, and then couldn't get a new nose because he was told that his library card was really for checking out free health insurance," explained Jack Honey Badger carefully.

"Huh?" said Mr. Taffle. He had tuned him out again; he just couldn't get over the fact that Jack Honey Badger had no nose. It was so weirdly yucky.

"So, now, when I cut off *your* nose, I'm going to eat it. Then, if you happen to sew it back on, you will always know that I pooped out your nose!" shouted Jack Honey Badger. He charged again, chopping his sword up and down in a syncopated rhythm that looked well-rehearsed. Mr. Taffle turned around, sprinted away through the tunnel, and nearly ran right off the top level of the bar. Just in time, he grabbed onto the banister on the edge of a staircase, which halted his momentum enough to keep him from falling to his death. Then the banister broke off the wall. "I think I'm going to fall to my death," he said as he fell to his certain death. Miraculously, the swinging cage that held the Disco Ball Alpaca had swung perfectly to scoop him up.

"What are the odds of that happening, dog?!" cheered Jack Honey Badger.

"What's wrong with you!" Mr. Taffle screamed back.

"Oh, you think I'm going to answer a question clearly asked to benefit your needs?" Jack Honey Badger backed up to get some running room and sprinted right off the edge of the staircase... but caught the bottom of the cage with just his middle and pointer finger. The Disco Ball Alpaca bit off those fingers and swallowed them. And Jack Honey Badger fell to his certain death... Nope. His fall was broken by a question mark shaped inflatable hot tub.

"What are the odds of that happening, dog?!"

The momentum caused the cage to swing wildly, which caused Mr. Taffle to also swing wildly, which caused him to accidentally swing his sword right though the wire holding the cage to the ceiling.

Thank God for Francine Carpenter, the previously mentioned intern, who also happened to be an ardent animal rights activist. Francine had passionately marched into the weekly boardroom meeting and insisted to the Director of Marketing that they install an emergency parachute onto the alpaca cage in case a freak accident occurred. The Director of Marketing took to heart Francine's passion for alpaca safety and cashed in a favor from the VP of Finance, which got him five minutes with the Duchess. The Duchess thought having a parachute on a cage was an idiotic idea. However, her on-call Tarot Card Reader had told her to scream "HECK YEAH" to any request asked on a Thursday, no matter what.

"I found the Duchess to be the total opposite of her reputation as the Antichrist," Francine would say whenever the subject of the Duchess was brought up.

Nevertheless, even with the cage parachute working perfectly, they still crashed hard enough on the ground for it to be classified as a medium-slow car crash. Mr. Taffle was launched right into a question mark love seat with big, puffy question mark pillows.

"WHAT ARE THE ODDS THAT THE ODDS ARE A BAG OF DOG CRAP, DOG?!"

Truth be told, Mr. Taffle actually felt quite cozy as he watched the Disco Ball Alpaca trot out of the now-ajar front door of the cage and begin to maul people like a rabid pit bull alpaca.

MAYHEM.

It was now a brutal stampede of femme fatales and non-VIPs! Mr. Taffle, still gripping onto his sword, sprang to his feet. "Where is The Mannequin Madam?!"

As he bullied his way through the pandemonium, Mr. Taffle witnessed a man dressed as the Flock of Seagulls guitar player wearing oversized sunglasses and lots of rouge on his cheeks. The man was continually shooting himself in the throat with his martini glass laser gun while loudly weeping that he still resented his stepdad for not treating him like his real son. Conditions were spiraling out of control. Mr. Taffle caught a glimpse of Monique the Mannequin in the reflection from the mirror behind the bar. There was no sign of The Mannequin Madam, but Monique stood safely against the wall. He turned and raced toward Monique, but the push of the crowd sent a wave of bodies crashing in Mr. Taffle's direction.

He met The Mannequin Madam's eyes through a small gap in the chaos. The gap was coincidentally shaped like an alpaca riding a unicycle.

"MANNEQUIN MADAM!" he screamed at the top of his lungs.

She heard him and screamed back, "MR. TAFFLE!"

Mr. Taffle jumped on top of the bar and sprinted toward her.

"HE'S FOUND ME!" she yelled, as she got sucked back into the crowd's powerful undertow.

Mr. Taffle dove off the bar into a sea of bodies. When he landed, there was Jack Honey Badger waiting for him as if, once again, he somehow knew Mr. Taffle would land right there.

"Yo-yo, what up, homie?" asked Jack Honey Badger, as he pressed his sword against Mr. Taffle's heart. "I'll take your car keys and wallet now."

Looking over Jack Honey Badger's shoulder, Mr. Taffle suddenly saw The Mannequin Madam, just as she was pulled around the corner by an arm in a long black sleeve with a bright white glove.

"Fine, just let me go now, please!" he said, handing over his wallet and keys.

"So, I got your wallet, I got your keys, and that means I got your car and your library card The only thing missing is your leather pants—"

WHAMMO!!!

The Disco Ball Alpaca barreled straight into Jack Honey Badger, which sent him flying 17 feet in the air. This time, he landed right on top of The Question Mark Mascot, who was in the grips of a fad diet addiction consisting of boiled water with lemon and A1 Steak Sauce. *Damn.*

Mr. Taffle bobbed and weaved around the corner in hot pursuit. There was no sign of The Mannequin Madam... and the giant question mark entrance on the wall was quickly closing. There was no way he was going to make it. But, deep down, he suspected he could make it if the pants wanted him to make it. So, he took a heroically stupid leap and... he didn't make it.

Mr. Taffle dangled outside the wall by one leg, with the other leg still stuck on the inside.

"Help me, The Wall!" begged Mr. Taffle to The Wall. The Wall emerged from the wall.

"Yeah, I guess this is what we get when I don't stick to the password policy," sighed The Wall, obviously pissed at himself. He begrudgingly took out the remote control and opened the question mark, which caused Mr. Taffle to fall hard to the ground. "Well, that was bound to happen, according to that thingy called gravity." There also could have been some additional nostril rotation from The Wall, but it was too hard to tell with the pricey face paint.

Mr. Taffle heard a car peeling out at the end of the block. It was the kind of peel-out that said, "We're kidnapping someone in a sports car, and we need to get as far away as possible as fast as possible."

Mr. Taffle haphazardly cut across the street. He was almost run over by a shiny silver 40-foot Winnebago with cherry-red lightning bolts painted on the sides. A man stuck his head out the driver's side window. This man looked exactly like... *OH DEAR LORD!*

CHAPTER NINE

The Fascinating History of the Farmer Ted 8s

Now, we all know the story of how the Pants of Insanity were created: Farmer loves cow with two udders, cow with two udders starts to pull practical jokes and perform gymnastics, Farmer slaughters cow with two udders moments after it conjures up a curse regarding the cows' quest to get as weird as possible.

However, to truly comprehend the gravity of the "OH, DEAR LORD" you just read at the end of the previous chapter, we must take it all the way back to the beginning and chronicle the historical timeline of the journey and adventures of Farmer Ted 1 and Farmer Ted 2.

FADE IN

"It was the 17th best summer ever in Lincoln Adjacent," joked Ted 1's parents in a deadpan style that Old Man "Mongoose" McGeester had once called genius. As a result, they never stopped saying it the entire summer.

And it was on the very last day of summer that Ted 1 and Ted 2, both impressively out of shape for being just freshly seven years old, became next-door neighbors. Although only a stone's throw away from each other, Ted 1's parents had a much more expensive house. To advertise they were much richer than anyone else in the neighborhood, they changed their building plans. Now, instead of building their planned tri-level back deck, they built a tri-level front deck. The front deck's crown jewel was a restaurant-sized wood-fire pizza oven. The huge oven was illuminated by a razzle-dazzle set of blinking lights that hung overhead and spelled out "PIZZA PARTY".

Although they had pizza-party weekends all summer, nobody had ever been invited after the Old Man "Mongoose" McGeester incident with the Ooni dough balls. But Ted 1 wouldn't stop shrieking (like the seven-year-old he was) that perhaps his new neighbor should be allowed to come over. This was really important to Ted 1, as he planned to steal and destroy Ted 2's Stretchy Octopus, which was dressed as a cowboy doll.

Ted 1 hadn't been able to stop thinking about the Stretchy Octopus since the moment he'd seen Ted 2 enjoying it while he was spying on him from inside of his closet, and then later from underneath his bed. So Ted 2 was finally allowed to come over and have one piece of pizza. He ate this as slowly as possible, per the advice of Old Man "Mongoose" McGeester.

This gave Ted 1 a perfect opportunity to snag the unattended Stretchy Octopus. The first thing he did was to slurp all the toxic jelly out. Ted 2 silently watched as Ted 1 proceeded to fall into a coma. Ted 1 would later claim that it was then—on the first night of his deep sleep—when he had his life-changing vision regarding world farming domination.

Ted 1's parents sued the monster corporation responsible for a majority stake in the company that manufactured the Stretchy Octopus. The corporation happened to be in the middle of merging with an even more ginormous conglomerate that insisted on more than one occasion that this record-breaking massive complex merger be *squeaky deaky* clean.

Ted 1 was awarded $1,679,435.87, in addition to company stock options, in order to keep the case quiet. This was easy for Ted 1, since he was in a coma. A copy of the corporation's check hung proudly above Ted 1's hospital bed in the most expensive picture frame available from the Lincoln Adjacent Drugstore, while he continued to pee out of a very expensive tube.

Ted 1's parents were so excited about their new financial fortune that they had totally spaced out about the very thing they had told Ted 1 a million times: "Never wrestle in the street after binge drinking." As a result of ignoring their own advice, Ted 1's parents were run over by a speeding truck and flattened in a manner very similar to their prized pizza dough. In accordance with their estate, Ted 1's parents were cremated in the wood pizza oven they had enjoyed so much.

"It was the 17th best cremation in the history of Lincoln Adjacent," announced Old Man "Mongoose" McGeester.

Ted 1 continued in his deep sleep for four years and 10 months, never knowing his parents had died while drunkenly celebrating all the cash he had made for them. When Ted 1 awoke from his coma, Ted 2 was right there with him. Ted 2 had made sure he would be the first to greet Ted 1 and tell him the tragic news of his parents' death. Revenge for the destruction of his Stretchy Octopus (dressed as a cowboy doll) would be so sweet!

"Ted 1, you're awake!" cheered Ted 2.

Ted 1 was totally discombobulated, trying to make sense of where he was and what had happened. Then he saw their reflections in the mirror. "Wowee, Ted 2! I'm way more handsome than you now, and in way better shape. What an amazing way to wake up."

It was true that having been on such a healthy liquid diet fed through a very expensive tube had caused Ted 1 to have the most impressive abdominal six pack of any 11-year-old in the world.

"Where are my parents?" yawned Ted 1 in a clearly non-drowsy way. It was a disinterested yawn. A yawn that said, "I could push you off a cliff on the way to lunch and still get lunch."

"Your parents were run over by a 1970 Dodge pickup driven by the character actor Phillip Tuffmo while crossing the street," blurted out Ted 2, exactly as he'd practiced all those times in the mirror. "Phillip is best known for having been Fish's pal in that show about the cops who like to roast each other with clever zingers!"

Ted 1 took in this news with a deep breath. Then he became deeply hungry, specifically deeply hungry for a BLT with avocado on lightly toasted pumpernickel bread. Farmer Ted 1 looked deeply into the pupils of Ted 2's eyes as if they were portals into his soul. "From this moment on, on my command, you will always make me a BLT with avocado, and always on lightly toasted pumpernickel bread."

Ted 2 tried to laugh it off, but he couldn't shake the feeling of a mental prison suddenly constricting around him. It felt like a storm of wet beach towels plunging down upon a field of daisies.

Ted 1 moved in with Ted 2's parents, as this had been Ted 1's parents' dying wish. This was a lie, but it was backed up by Old

Man "Mongoose" McGeester. Ted 2's parents had always called Ted 2 by the name Ted 1 because, of course, he was their one and only Ted 1.

However, when Ted 2's family moved into Ted 1's much more posh house and started using their famous wood fire pizza oven, they delicately broached the subject with Ted 2 of changing his name. They asked if they might start calling Ted 1... Ted 1... to avoid confusion, and also because Ted 1's settlement had grown to $25,872,914.87 due to the stock options he had been rewarded in the payoff from the monstrosity subsidiary of the corporation.

Ted 2 agreed to be demoted from Ted 1 to Ted 2, even though, in reality, it had already been decided. Coincidentally, his left eye twitch issue began the following day.

"Of course this is coincidental," said his school counselor on the day he finally poured the whiskey directly into the bowl of Frosted Mini Wheats. "You have to eat them foggy... soggy or what's the damn point."

Tragically, Ted 2's parents would pass away from complications brought by an icky case of hepatitis they had contracted while participating in Hands Across America. Apparently, the *wash your hands after going to the bathroom* government-sponsored jingle, constantly playing on all three major TV networks and a few unbelievably critical FM stations in powerful key markets, hadn't really worked that well.

In accordance with their estate, Ted 2's parents were also cremated in the wood pizza oven that they had enjoyed so much. "It was the 18th best cremation in the history of Lincoln Adjacent," announced Old Man "Mongoose" McGeester.

Ted 1's plan of becoming a farming legend was put into action immediately upon receiving the cash on the morning of his 18th birthday. Of course, his best friend—his "brother from another run-over-and-cremated-in-a-pizza-oven mother"—would be his right-hand man. From this moment on, their official names would be changed to Farmer Ted 1 and Farmer Ted 2.

It was actually Farmer Ted 2 who came up with the suggestion that Farmer Ted 1 go and network with the most elite movers and shakers in the farming game at the big Farm Aid Concert happening in Austin, Texas. The only problem was that Farmer Ted 1 hated country music, as well as the idea of giving his money away to any-one for any reason. But he could try to pretend that he enjoyed both of these activities. To get into character, he constantly repeated to himself, "I really do support the cause of helping non-foreign farm-ers while slamming well whiskey all day."

Thus, Farmer Ted 1 would *coincidentally* be able to hobnob with the movers and shakers in the second-tier VIP backstage area. And of course, Farmer Ted 2—the ace in his never-ending hole—was coming with him to party it up. However, Farmer Ted 1 insisted that Farmer Ted 2 wear the name-brand ear plugs that guaranteed complete deafness during the concert at all times. It was equally vital that Farmer Ted 2 never look at the stage or at the jumbotron for the entire show. This was almost as crucial as figuring out how to prepare Farmer Ted 1's BLT-with-avocado-on-lightly-toasted-pumpernickel sandwich during the performance while simulta-neously participating in the do-si-do pit that Farmer Ted 2 was required to start every 9 minutes.

The networking, however, was a total bust, due to the fact that Farmer Ted 1 was in the top 1% of the crappiest personalities of all time. But then, Farm Aid's lone rock n' roller, Sammy Hagar, took the stage and declared to all, "I Can't Drive 55!"

Farmer Ted 1 shouted back at Sammy Hagar as loud as he could, "I Can't Drive 62!" He was determined to get whatever kicks he could out of this event, so why not unleash some of his deadpan comic talent like Old Man "Mongoose" McGeester had always encouraged him to do?

Then the most unexpected thing happened: Farmer Ted 1 heard the sound of genuine laughter. (Farmer Ted 2 didn't hear the genuine laughter, as he couldn't hear a sound with the name-brand earplugs jammed into his ear holes.) This laughter came from a middle aged Japanese man named Banzan Kubo. He was wearing a gold sequin cowboy hat with 8 LED lights that illuminated the brim of the hat. He just purchased the hat at the Farm Aid merch booth. He reeked of well whisky. As it happened, Banzan was also attempting to penetrate into the who's who of powerbroker farmer tycoons in order to pitch his scientific breakthrough that would change the farming game forever.

CHAPTER TEN

The Fascinating History of the Farmer Ted 8s

Part 2: Banzan Screws Up

Banzan was a man of science, but not actually a scientist, as he was thrown out of his university for a series of attacks at the *too-cool-for-school dorm shower misunderstanding*. However, it was in Banzan's darkest hour of shame when a good-energy creativity waterfall appeared and poured down on him constantly, even when he was showering. Banzan was well aware that nobody else could see this relentless waterfall stalking him. So, to prove it was real, and to make it stop, he held a plugged-in toaster up in the air to demonstrate that he would get electrocuted. But instead of getting zapped, he received a series of divine chemical equations and numerical sexy whispers. Banzan decided right there to dedicate his life to navigating through this divine puzzle, as his intuition told him it would somehow get him filthy rich. Unfortunately, only hours later Banzan was arrested for a chemical explosion at the *too-cool-for-school aquarium store misunderstanding.*

After a brutal 19 years and seven days in prison, and with only one minute before he was set to be released, he finally accepted that he would never be able to solve this divine puzzle. Instead, he thought that perhaps he should switch gears and focus on that thingy that he'd whipped up a few days previously: an idea for cloning cows so they would be born with two sets of udders.

"Twice the pulling, but twice the milk!" Banzan sang, just like the commercial jingle made by the advertising team that brought you Mentos and Fascism. This was followed by a milking-hand gesture that made it appear that he was hitchhiking with broken elbows.

"Have you submitted your cloning formula to Nate, Sue, Sandy, or Dean at the USDA main hub in Richmond?" Farmer Ted 1 sneered at Banzan.

"As a matter of fact, I have," Banzan sneered back. "And yes, I have been rejected by Mitch, Sue, and Sandy. I'm still waiting on Dean, but Dean is Dean, right? However, I have an alternate plan that involves a thing I like to call... The Underground Farms of the Two-Udder Cows."

"Well, I just happen to have compromising pictures of Dean with Sue and Nate, as well as millions of dollars to invest," Farmer Ted 1 sneered back to Banzan.

AND SO, IT BEGAN...

However, only a few months after the first of The Underground Farms of the Two-Udder Cows was constructed, Banzan would claim that he was totally fried from life in the farm fast lane. Truth be told, he was bummed out that the farms couldn't have attention drawn to them. They had to keep a low profile due to the fact that, despite the approval of the USDA, they were still super duper sketchy. That's why the underground farms resembled the secret meth lab from Breaking Bad. And because of this lack of publicity, he would never get credit for his amazing discovery and all the perks that would have come along with being famous. He found being rich without being famous felt like having feet for hands. It was time to go home.

Banzan moved back home to Fukushima, where he became addicted both to huffing three-eyed fish carcasses and to watching reruns of the third season of *Saturday Night Live*. He always focused specifically on the sketch where regular SNL host Steve Martin and full-time Not Ready for Prime Time Players cast member Dan Aykroyd played the The Wild and Crazy Guys. These were the Czechoslovakian brothers named Yortuk and Georg Festrunk, who dressed in loud, obnoxious outfits. The pair liked to catcall foxy American women with loud, obnoxious one-liners commenting on their large breasts. This would always lead to their catchphrase, "*We are two wild and crazy guys!*"

One night while Banzan was sucking out the tumor from a koi fish's eyeball, this catchphrase made him laugh so hard that he spat out the fisheye. It flew across the room and broke the glass of his trophy case. This caused the entire row of his Kyomai dancing-participation trophies to shatter. As he swept up the trophy glass, he saw a reflection of his horrifically chapped lips. His lips began sexily whispering to him the same unsolvable chemical equations and numerical secrets that had originally been broadcast to him as a youth. He took another long suck from the koi's eyeball, just to really take it in, while he hatched a master plan. He would travel back to the United States of America and kidnap Steve Martin and Dan Aykroyd!

Boom!

You see, he had realized that hidden in the whispering numerical equation was the longitude and latitude coordinates that perfectly pinpointed the section of the human brain that produced punch-line zingers. He would clone Martin and Aykroyd using the same principles he had used for the two-udder cows. These clones would be fearless, with no conscience, and they would catch their enemies off guard with their superior comic timing. They would also be masters in the science and the art of Japanese pickling like he was. *Because daddy deserves that.* But did he really need both Steve Martin and Dan Aykroyd to achieve all of this? (He didn't want to be rude about it, but he could allow Aykroyd to continue to blow people's minds by reminding them he was actually the skinny Blues Brother.)

Banzan arrived unannounced at his old business partner Farmer Ted 1's Malibu McMansion summer home. There he could crash at the guest villa, and this would serve as his home base.

Now, everybody knew that Steve Martin played the banjo so darn good that he could actually make people come out to watch someone play the banjo (even though everyone in attendance was secretly praying he would pull out a rubber chicken and recite lines from *The Jerk*).

So, Banzan hid in the bushes in front of the only banjo shop in Los Angeles and waited every day for Steve Martin to show up to buy banjo supplies. After waiting there daily for eight months and four days, Banzan finally realized Steve Martin probably ordered his banjo supplies online or got an assistant to pick them up for him. He also realized that this part of the plan had perhaps been hatched as a side effect of his huffing those toxic fish eyeballs.

This failure was yet another major stumbling block in Banzan's quest to be famous. He needed to find someone who possessed unique comedy stylings similar to Martin or Aykroyd so he could clone them at his castle during a lightning storm.

That evening, Banzan and Farmer Ted 1 were relaxing in his rooftop infinity pool, watching Farmer Ted 2 play his favorite game: "Farmer Ted 2 Hog-tied to the Diving Board." Farmer Ted 1 slurped a cup of curdled milk and promptly projectile-vomited a puddle of peas and corn directly into Farmer Ted 2's face. "Um, you got something on your lip," zinged Farmer Ted 1 with bull's-eye comic timing.

At that moment, Banzan realized that the answer had been right in front of him the entire time! Farmer Ted 1 had a unique whip-smart comedy style that could generate the same buffoonery effect perfect for distracting an enemy. He was the ideal candidate for a killing comedy machine.

Banzan walked out of the room, returned with a George Foreman Grill, smacked Farmer Ted 1 over the head with it, and took him prisoner. Finally, Farmer Ted 2 was set free from Farmer Ted 1's control, as he served zero purpose to Banzan's cloning plans. This actually turned out to be a major miscalculation by Banzan, which honestly should have easily been red-flagged considering Farmer Ted 2's "Stockholm Syndrome" right ankle tattoo. Farmer Ted 2 couldn't handle it on the outside and took up skydiving to help him get used to all the kooky freedom. However, Farmer Ted 2 had secretly replaced his own parachute with stuffed animal stingrays, fresh daisies and a wet beach towel. The remains of Farmer Ted 2's body were sent back to his hometown of Lincoln Adjacent.

"It was the 19th best cremation in the history of Lincoln Adjacent," announced Old Man "Mongoose" McGeester.

Unfortunately, many of the key details that logged the progression of Farmer Ted 1's cloning had been, for some reason, neatly and deliberately cut out from the scroll on which they had been recorded. Yes, it was all written on a scroll. As Banzan had always said, "Any document really worth a damn was written on a scroll."

Day 7: Farmer Ted 1 won't stop screaming, which is making it hard to hear The Wild and Crazy Guys' catchphrase on loop. I think he either despises this catchphrase or the clamps keeping his eyes open could have been designed with maybe some padding. Frankly, I'm a bit nervous about starting the Solid Gold Dancer montage. I have a sneaky suspicion that it may make him swallow his own tongue.

Day 8: Farmer Ted 1 tried to swallow his own tongue.

Day 398: Farmer Ted 1 has been begging repeatedly for a BLT with avocado on lightly toasted pumpernickel, so I finally gave in and made him one. And then he wouldn't eat it! Turns out it has to be made by Farmer Ted 2 or he literally can't digest it. What a waste of time. Yo, pal, Farmer Ted 2 was splattered on top of an unsuspecting pack of geese. It was horrible and very gross. Accept it and move on damnit.

Day 978: Farmer Ted 1 finally started to talk with a Czechoslovakian accent! Hahahahaha, he's already so much funnier. Hahahahaha, I'm very optimistic. Hahahahaha, I think he just tried to swallow his own tongue again.

Day 1009: Dear diary, why do I enjoy not flushing the toilet in a public bathroom? Wait, this isn't my diary. Can you erase in a scroll?

Day 1234: I've inserted the two-udder cow's uterus into Farmer Ted 1's colon. Now, all I need is the lightning storm magnet to work tomorrow night, and I think we could be in business.

Day 1235: The lightning storm magnet is a giant piece of crap, now impaled inside of the tree trunk fountain in my mediation garden.

Day 2,390: A massive lightning storm finally happened! So, I wrapped Farmer Ted 1 in aluminum foil and tied him to the satellite dish on top of the castle roof. Truth is, I never used that satellite anymore, so I didn't really care if it got damaged. All I really need is YouTube on my laptop, and I'm good. Anyway, two bolts of lightning hit him simultaneously! So, now I've got him back down in his Iron Maiden waiting for results. I'll keep you posted.

Day 2,392: There have been no results, and I'm getting slightly concerned that Farmer Ted 1 might not make it, considering that his always-impressive six pack of abs has blown up into six pustulating tumors. And it's just so tempting to pop them.

Day 2,393: I popped them! I couldn't help myself. And then six fetuses, each with fully formed legs, kicked their way out of his abdominal tumors. I can't find them anywhere... yet I hear them uncontrollably cackling. But there's a sadness in those cackles.

Day 2,394: Farmer Ted 1 is dead. Actually, he died yesterday. I just forgot to mention it. Weird, since I hated his guts and should be happy. But I feel sad. No, I'm happy.

Day 2,400: I finally saw one of the fetuses running across the kitchen counter carrying a full jar of Sunomono pickles it stole from the refrigerator. I couldn't catch it, but I saw its face. And it was the face of Farmer Ted 1! It worked! Now, I must figure out a way to trap the fetus Farmer Teds so I can begin their training.

Day 2401: Well, the trap didn't work. I'm now locked in this man cave with only this scroll, a pack of 300 miniaturized plastic action soldiers, and a half-chewed pack of watermelon Bubble Yum gum. I fear the Farmer Ted fetuses now want to eat me—as they just tried to eat me.

Day 2402: The Farmer Ted 1 fetuses can now talk, and they're telling jokes. But they're still in the adolescent phase of their comedy, so right now all their material is literally baby humor. "What did the pee pee say to the poo poo? Do me a solid and drop by the pool when it starts to rain." The fetuses laughed at this joke uncontrollably for over nine hours.

What have I done?

Day 2404: I'm down to my last piece of Bubble Yum, and I'm afraid this very well may be my final entry in the scroll. The fetuses have told me that they're going to call themselves the Farmer Ted 6ers. But I reminded them that, as there had been two Farmer Teds before them, this would be disrespectful. I was pleasantly surprised when they agreed.

They would be the Farmer Ted 8s, even though we all also agreed that "Farmer Ted 6ers" had a way better flow to it. They then informed me it was crucial that they consume my flesh in the next 15 minutes, and that they had found my power saw. And on that note, don't ever stop believing in yourself. The universe is magical, man!

CHAPTER ELEVEN
Barb Was Right

"Hey, Sword Guy! What are you doing with a sword?" asked Farmer Ted 3, an exact duplicate of Farmer Ted 1, in a fake Czechoslovakian accent. He tried not to crack up as he leaned his head farther out the Winnebago window in order to show off the perfect circular bald spot on the top of his head. He had an additional smaller circular bald spot to the right of it and an even smaller dot to the left.

"A woman's been kidnapped! They're getting away!" Mr. Taffle desperately screamed. He pointed at a 1977 black Trans Am speeding away up the street in the distance. *The car was a tribute to Burt*

Reynolds from the film Smokey and the Bandit *(and our second reference to the Macho Mustache Man Perm Hall of Famer).*

Farmer Ted 4 stuck his head out of the driver's window. "Well, get in, Sword Guy!"

Mr. Taffle dropped his sword and hopped onto a service elevator on the left side of the Winnebago, where he was lifted to a second-level doorway and then promptly yanked inside.

Farmer Teds 5 through 8 were all exact clones, the only difference being that they were each dressed in contrasting variations of the tight plaid pants and loud, unbuttoned shirts of the The Wild and Crazy Guys' wardrobe. They all wore the same large medallions emblazoned with a portrait depicting Banzan Kubo at the exact moment they had eaten him alive, back when they were just fetuses. In fact, the entire inside of the Winnebago was a shrine to Banzan's castle. Jars of unopened Sunomonoes and plastic Tupperware containers filled with wasabi were stacked on rows of meditation alter shelves that ran along the Winnebago walls. A large statue of the eight-headed Yamata no Orochi dragon was placed directly in the middle of the aisle, which really messed up the entire recreational vehicle's feng shui. Not to mention that a person had to squish uncomfortably against the Winnebago's pantry in order to just get past it. The symbolic representation of this eight-headed dragon to the Farmer Ted 8s was pretty obvious. However, it was the actual Tree Truck Rainfall Fountain, with the lightning-storm magnet still impaled in it, that was the crown jewel of the entire Winnebago—narrowly beating out the electronic toilet seats. The toilet seats had outlets to charge a phone or tablet, and they sprayed up a measured vanilla bean-scented stream of water, based on a person's weight.

The Winnebago sped after the Trans Am and gained on it surprisingly fast. This speed was possible because the Winnebago engine was specially built by a master automotive engine designer, who was rated the easiest to kidnap without having to drive more than a hundred miles by their secretary Barb. Mr. Taffle charged to the front of the Winnebago. He looked out into the mid-century-bamboo-with-gold-trim driver's side mirror and caught a glimpse of Monique the Mannequin lying face down in an intersecting alley.

Poor Monique, thought Mr. Taffle. It was one and a half-seconds later when he realized he was feeling bad for a mannequin, while an actual real woman's life was in danger.

"Go faster!" yelled Mr. Taffle.

Suddenly, all six of the Farmer Ted 8s simultaneously erupted into a fit of furious cackling. The Farmer Ted 8s operated on one hive mind, which was actually very similar to the way My Best Friend and the rest of the two-udder cows had operated before they had been slaughtered. It really didn't make a difference which one of the Farmer Ted 8s was talking, as they were really just one voice coming from six different mouths.

"I've got an idea!"

"Shut your mouth!"

"Just one word!"

"Shut your mouth!"

"It will be quick!"

"Shut your mouth!"

"Harpoon gun!"

"You're a genius!"

Farmer Ted 5 bolted to the back of the Winnebago, skillfully vaulted over the statue of the Yamata no Orochi dragon, and returned with a harpoon gun the size of a rocket launcher.

"Wait, I'm not positive I saw her get in this car—"

"IT'S IMPERATIVE WE ARE POSITIVE!" shouted Farmer Ted 5 as he opened the driver's side door. "Who wants to hold onto my feet?"

"Me!"

"Me!"

"Me!"

"Me!"

"Me!"

Farmer Ted 5 dangled out the door, holding the harpoon gun and aiming it at the car, now only 300 yards away. All the other Farmer Teds held onto his feet, including Farmer Ted 3, who had casually left the Winnebago to drive itself, which it amazingly did.

"Who's driving?!" screamed Mr. Taffle as he leaped over the driver's side seat, desperately grabbing onto the steering wheel right before they ran off the road.

"I'm guessing you are now."

"Is this a trick question?"

"I forgot to study."

"And I can't remember where my classroom is."

"Why am I at school naked?!"

"Stop! It's too risky to shoot that harpoon gun," ordered Mr. Taffle.

"I agree! I need a countdown!" ordered Farmer Ted 5.

"It's my turn!"

"No, it's not"

"You're always lying"

"I am always lying!" realized Farmer Ted 5, taking a moment to reflect.

Mr. Taffle slammed on the brakes but... "The brakes aren't working!"

"Barb told us to fix the brakes!"

"Screw Barb!"

"Barb was right!"

"Apologies to Barb!"

"I need a countdown!"

"Please, don't shoot!" begged Mr. Taffle.

"Copy that!"

"Three!"

"Two!"

"One and a half!"

"NOOOOOOOOOOO!" screamed Mr. Taffle.

Sarah Varga, a tattoo artist who had a work/live in space in the newly remodeled Downtown Lofts, happened to be looking out the window when the harpoon was shot from the Winnebago. This is the statement she gave the police: "I'm sorry, but you've been misinformed. I didn't see anything."

However, a local police officer named Emme Pulous went rogue and continued the investigation by going undercover and getting tattooed so she could get information out of the tattoo artist. The problem was that Officer Pulous was totally broke, due to her addiction of hoarding automatic weapons. So in order to be able to afford a tattoo, she agreed to participate in the 50% off sale; this bought her a brand new design the tattoo shop was promoting.

The following was taken straight from their recorded conversation:

So, I just happened to be staring out the window, brainstorming about improvements to this new tattoo design involving duplicate nipples tattooed directly under the real nipples called "blurry nipps" that you're going to love. It really could become the next tramp stamp, maybe... I don't know. Anyway, that's when I saw a Smokey and the Bandit replica Trans Am barreling down the road, being chased by this super-fast Winnebago with lightning stripes on the side. Then I noticed some dude dressed in a wacky suit dangling out the driver's side door with this massive rifle! But it's not a rifle. It's a harpoon gun! He fired a harpoon at the Trans Am! Now, according to the second rule of the three laws of motion, force is equal to the change in momentum over time, which is mass times velocity. So, it made zero mathematical sense that when the Winnebago harpoon made a direct hit to the Trans Am, it would be the Winnebago that shot completely around the hookah bar across the street. The Trans Am didn't move an inch, even though it's a stone-cold fact that an object will remain at rest or in a uniform state of motion unless that state is changed by an external force. This also went completely against the first rule of the three laws of motion. The harpoon rope then broke apart, and the Winnebago flipped wildly out of control. I didn't count, but I'm guessing it flipped like seven times! This actually put my mind a little at ease, as it made sense: for every action in nature there is an equal and opposite reaction, which is the third rule of the three laws of motion. But maybe the craziest part of the entire thing was that the Winnebago somehow ended up landing on all four wheels and then just casually drove off as if nothing had happened. This obviously proved without a doubt the existence of Jesus Christ.

Luckily, Mr. Taffle had had the foresight to put on his seatbelt right before the harpoon was fired. He took a moment to regain his composure and examined his body to make sure he was indeed still in one piece. But why was he mostly relieved that his pants hadn't been damaged? Now he felt a dire urge to lightly apply olive oil to any small tears that might have occurred, as that was the best way to repair leather... *Wait, how did he even know this?*

As he shook himself from his little reverie, he realized that the Farmer Ted 8s had disappeared. Where the hell had they gone? Had they somehow all been launched out of the Winnebago during one of the flips? Honestly, he didn't care what happened to them. They reminded him of circus clowns. And everyone knows the only thing creepier than clowns are mimes. All Mr. Taffle really cared about at that moment was the well-being of the pants. So, he looked down at them once again to make double sure they were okay. That's when he realized what had happened to the Farmer Ted 8s. All six of them were jammed under his seat, staring up at him. They had been waiting patiently for him to realize they were staring up at him so they could finally…"SWOOOOOOOOOOOORD GUY!"

They ripped off the driver's seat, launching Mr. Taffle in the air, and proceeded into an all-out celebratory wrestling scrum. After exactly eight seconds, all the Farmer Ted 8s stopped wrestling at the exact same time due to their shared internal stopwatch that regulated these violent celebratory scrums. Then an internal monitor alerted them that they were in desperate need to hydrate with a bag of juice in a gravity-free environment.

Mr. Taffle found himself floating in a chamber designed to be a replica of the Milky Way galaxy. Now, normally getting to hover around in simulated cosmos would be something appealing to Mr. Taffle, considering that he had dreamt about being an astronaut as a kid. But he had ditched that dream after his mother suggested that being an astronaut would be a perfect job for him if only he were a lot smarter and not such a chicken about almost everything.

Mr. Taffle was desperate for the Farmer Ted 8s' help, as Jack Honey Badger had stolen his keys and wallet. And while it was now certain that the Farmer Ted 8s were a never-ending deranged cartoon come to life, he knew that if he could just figure out a way to apply the lessons he had learned from the *How to Turn a Small Group of Friends Into Your Cult* TED Talk from Mr. Manley, they could actually be useful to him.

An astronaut waiter floated over, carrying a tray on which were bags of assorted juices. The Farmer Teds grabbed their juices as if this was the only reason they ever came here (which it always was).

"This bag of juice deserves an award for best bag of juice," said Farmer Ted 5 as he slurped from the bag.

"But we don't get any awards tonight. We failed the Sword Guy. And I blame everyone but me."

"I'm the one who missed the tail pipe!"

"And I'm the one who told you to aim into the tail pipe!"

"And I'm the one who stayed silent when I knew that you had absolutely zero chance of hitting the tail pipe!"

"Silent but deadly!"

"The one who smelt it dealt it!"

Mr. Taffle decided to call The Mannequin Madam. He rang her three times in a row, but she wasn't answering.

"How are we going to save my girlfriend?!" pleaded Mr. Taffle, realizing he didn't mean to call her his girlfriend, but not feeling the need to correct himself.

"Sword Guy has a sweetheart?!"

"Sword Guy has a sweetheart and a girlfriend?!"

"How do you manage the jealousy that must arise from that dynamic?"

Mr. Taffle's suspense-jingle ringtone interrupted. He recognized the number.

"It's her!" He quickly put on his Projecto headband and answered. The Mannequin Madam hologram appeared, causing each startled Farmer Ted 8 to yank hard onto the crown of hair of whatever Farmer Ted was floating to the left of them.

"The Mannequin Madam! Thank God you're all right! Where are you?"

The Mannequin Madam's projection whipped around quickly, looking out to see if someone was coming. "I dropped Monique in the alleyway behind The Truth," she said urgently. "Check her secret pouch—" The transmission cut off.

"I NEED YOU GUYS TO DRIVE ME TO FIND THAT MANNEQUIN RIGHT NOW PLEASE!" demanded Mr. Taffle, but politely.

"I need to find me one of those magical headbands right now please!" politely demanded the Farmer Ted 8s in unison.

I should probably call the police and have them meet us there, thought Mr. Taffle out loud as he swam down to the ground. Farmer Ted 4 grabbed Mr. Taffle's pant leg and pulled him right back up.

"Well, there's an idea."

"Could be a bad idea?"

"Could be an idea that gets your bag of juice taken away," said Farmer Ted 5 as he took away Mr. Taffle's bag of juice.

"Why is that a bad idea?" wondered Mr. Taffle.

"Great question!"

"Multiple choice?"

"Great idea!"

"Return his bag of juice!" Farmer Ted 5 handed back Mr. Taffle's bag of juice.

"A, if you call the cops, you will have to tell them about us, and we'll be forced to eject you out of VIP."

"B, if you call the cops, they might very well figure out we just robbed a traveling circus, and we'll be obliged to scratch you off the guest list."

"C, if you call the cops, the Kodiak bear that rides on a unicycle who's locked in Barb's dungeon might not get his salmon snack on time, and then we'd be compelled to downgrade you to coach."

"D, if you call the cops... Everything already as explained in A, B, and C, so, you know... I'm done." Farmer Ted 5 leaned over and whispered in Mr. Taffle's ear.

"FYI, the SAT study tutorials for the privileged say to always guess B or C if you don't know the answer."

"And now your final answer, The Sword Guy?" the Farmer Ted 8s said in unison. Tension filled the room and, this time, each Farmer Ted 8 grabbed onto the hair of the Farmer Ted to the *right* of them. Finally...

"E. All of the above," confidently answered Mr. Taffle.

The Farmer Ted 8s proceeded directly into a full synchronized gravity-free swimming routine; it was a tribute to the Solid Gold Dancers performing to the 5 top songs of 1981. They had been working on this routine every time they had a post-scrum celebration at the Outer Space Juice Bar, which by now was 673 days in a row. And if you knew how hard they worked at it (not to mention how it had been brainwashed into their subconscious), then you wouldn't really have been impressed at all. It was very amateurish, especially with Farmer Ted 6 being distractingly out of sync almost the entire performance.

"You are not correct," they said in perfect unison as they ended the routine, except for Farmer Ted 6, who was still off by a good half-second. Farmer Ted 5 once again whispered in Mr. Taffle's ear.

"E was the correct answer, but after consulting with myself, I was forced to rule that since E wasn't given as a choice you're going to be escorted out of the gold member lounge and promptly murdered."

"Wait! I promise that I'm not going to tell the police anything about you guys," promised Mr. Taffle.

"They always say that."

"They always do say that!" realized Farmer Ted 5.

"Say it!"

"Don't spray it!"

Mr. Taffle realized he better *Learning to Fly like Tom Petty, yo,* or he was going to be dead meat. "Now listen, gentleman. I believe with all my heart and soul that breaking up our partnership at this time would be a major-league whopper of a mistake!" he said with a salesman's enthusiasm. "And I'm not just saying that because of the circumstances. THIS IS IMPORTANT! We undeniably make an amazing team. But it's more than that. You see, I don't have a lot of friends, and I was really feeling hopeful, not to mention grateful, that we were becoming fast friends. If I've learned anything in this crazy life it's that friendship is something rare and should be cherished. YOU DON'T MESS WITH THAT! IT'S SACRED!"

"We have become friends."

"I'd pick you up from the airport on Friday at rush hour."

"I'd help you move a heavy dresser down a preposterously precarious spiral staircase."

"I'd let you make out with Barb."

Farmer Ted 5 leaned over and whispered in Mr. Taffle's ear, "It's a hot take to think your hot sauce is hot enough to be our hot sauce, hot shot."

"It's more than hot enough," cockily snapped Mr. Taffle, who quickly pinched his left nipple. Thank God the Farmer Ted 8s didn't know any of The Taffle Tells.

"It'll be our first initiation ceremony!"

"Since the last one!"

"Since the screamer!"

"Don't call him that!"

"Since the yeller!"

"He was my favorite!"

"Stop lying!"

"I *am* always lying," realized Farmer Ted 5 as he grabbed Mr. Taffle by both eyebrows and pulled him toward the exit. Mr. Taffle didn't notice Jack Honey Badger spying on him from behind a floating cluster of subatomic particles. Jack Honey Badger then proceeded to calmly spray his bag of juice up his left nostril until the entire bag was drained.

As they got back into the Winnebago, Mr. Taffle furiously brainstormed about how to convince them to hold off this initiation so he could retrieve the mannequin. But as the Winnebago's interior transformed into a luxurious movie theater, he didn't like his chances. And, truth be told, he was pretty blown away when the Yamata no Orochi dragon transformed into a popcorn machine. Not to mention when the oil painting of the god of war Hachimchi (putting the god of rice and agriculture Inari Okami in a headlock) transformed into a movie screen with a classic red velvet curtain. He almost said out loud, *That's super neat!* But by then he was in full sales mode. The kind of mode that theoretically was primed to ignite the *sizzle*.

"Fellas, it's imperative we don't waste another second! We need to get to that mannequin before someone scoops her up and puts her in their driver's side seat so they can drive in the carpool lane without getting a ticket."

"What a marvelous scheme!"

"You're diabolically cunning!"

"Think of the time we'd save driving to corporate headquarters!"

"But the Founding Fathers would never allow it!"

"And since we are the Founding Fathers, that makes more sense than anything else I can think of."

"Start the film," ordered Farmer Ted 6, as he tossed Mr. Taffle a gym bag filled with popcorn that leaked out gooey butter from the top.

As the lights dimmed, the curtain parted, and Farmer Ted 5 appeared on the screen. He was dressed in the same outfit he was currently wearing: a school-bus yellow crushed velvet tight suit and with the paisley blue handkerchief tied around his neck.

"Welcome insert initiate's name here. We're so delighted you decided to unleash your true self and transform into one of us! Just remember, the safe word is… there is no safe word. Almost all of us think you're going to do great, except for the swimming portion. And this is the part where you get a standing ovation."

The Farmer Ted 8s stood up and applauded for eight seconds. The Farmer Ted 5 on the screen continued. "Now, let's get you up to speed on the most important thing you're going to need to know about your transformation into a Farmer Ted 8. We are in a constant turf war with the Fun-sized Norse Warriors that takes place every day except Tuesday. And that's only because of a clerical error by Barb. This will be on the written part of the exam, and for God's sake, wipe that cocky look off my face. Now, take it away, cocky Farmer Ted 5 in present time."

"Thank you me," said the present-time Farmer Ted 5 as he read off a deck of rainbow flashcards.

"Insert initiate's name here…Sword Guy or *The* Sword Guy… Let's go with just Sword Guy."

"Except he's a sword guy without a sword."

"A swordless sword guy."

"That's an oxymoron, moron."

"Not the direction I'd go in if I was a sword guy."

"Perhaps we should just skip right to the flying glowing orb part of the ceremony," said the Farmer Ted 5 on the screen.

"You're always right about everything, pre-recorded Farmer Ted 5, and I'm jealous of myself for that," replied Farmer Ted 5 as he flipped a switch on the arm of his theater chair. And, dramatically, a flashing blue orb slowly flew toward Mr. Taffle from the back of the Winnebago.

"And now, Sword Guy, prepare to face your first test," said Farmer Ted 5 as he waited for something to happen. "I said, prepare to meet your first test."

Finally…

"It's busted again." Interrogation-style bright lights turned on, revealing that the orb was actually hanging from some fishing line attached to the far end of the Winnebago.

"Technical difficulties!"

"I blame Barb!"

"You're a Barb blamer!"

"I am a Barb blamer," realized Farmer Ted 5. "But since Barb isn't here ONCE AGAIN to fix the flying pulsating orb, then I nominate myself."

Farmer Ted 5 calmly walked over to the orb, proceeded to stomp it eight times, and then calmly picked out a pair of hair clippers from inside the destroyed globe.

"Now prepare to meet the Farmer Ted 8s' ceremonial hair clippers," said the Farmer Ted 5 on the screen.

One thing was now certain, Mr. Taffle would soon have the three-circle haircut that represents all three circles of life: Professional, Family, and Fun. He needed a miracle. And then… KAAAABLAAAAAAAAAAAAAM!!!!!!!!!!!!!

That miracle arrived in the form of Jack Honey Badger, now armed with Mr. Taffle's Katana sword. He exploded through the top of the roof as though he had just jumped off a 25-foot bridge above them—which was exactly what had happened. The force of the fall made the sword fly out of Jack Honey Badger's hands, slicing right through one of the plastic Tupperware containers filled with wasabi.

Now, who doesn't like those animal vs. animal hypothetical showdowns. You know the ones that speculate who would win in a fight if, for instance, a western lowland gorilla fought a leopard. Would the gorilla's tremendous physical strength and intelligence overcome the agility and predatory instincts of the feline stealth hunter?

Nope.

But in this edition of animal vs. animal, it's actually a much harder matchup to predict. Could a human rabid honey badger really take out a pack of six perfect comedy clone fighting machines that laugh like hyenas? And let's just go ahead and call the Farmer Ted 8s "the hyenas" for the following fight sequence to really milk all of the fun and hyper violence.

Jack Honey Badger instantaneously zeroed in on Mr. Taffle's pants and lunged for them. Then, suddenly, everything went into slow motion for Mr. Taffle. He had dreamt in slow motion many times, and his online robot therapist had said this meant he felt powerless, anxious, and/or frustrated. But in this case, he had more than a sneaking suspicion the pants were somehow responsible.

Mr. Taffle easily snagged the ceremonial hair clippers, shoved them in Jack Honey Badger's mouth, and blasted his teeth like an electric toothbrush attached to a jet motor. This caused Jack Honey Badger to collapse back into three of the hyenas, who already had their taser guns drawn.

What?!...Hyenas with tasers!

ZAP! ZAP! ZAP AND ZAP!

Unfortunately for the hyenas, Honey Badger actually enjoyed being tased, because of course Honey Badger liked it. In addition, it somehow gave him super-villain strength.

A WHIRLWIND OF VIOLENT CHAOS! *And now, one would suspect that, in this episode of Honey Badger Vs. Gang of hyenas, the winner would be any hyena that could make it out of the Winnebago alive.* But Mr. Taffle didn't stick around to see the winner. Although he was still extremely curious to witness the outcome, he snuck out the side door.

Mr. Taffle sprinted away from the Winnebago while hissing the *sizzle* as if perhaps this would make him run faster. While it didn't make him run faster, it did pump up his confidence. He was going to escape. He was going to save The Mannequin Madam. He was going to call his mother. No, his mother already had a negative bias against Katrina, considering that she'd had to hear about his heart being pulverized by her daily. He would have to bite the bullet and call Mr. Manley, even though Mr. Manley had advised him to never bother him during off-hours without a to-be-determined donation of sketchy crypto.

While continuing to run up the steep, hilly street, Mr. Taffle slid on the Projecto headgear. He managed to flip through his phone contacts without breaking stride.

Mr. Manley's projection, dressed in a swimming attire (which included a swim cap, goggles, snorkel, and water wings) and holding up his familiar pinwheel, appeared in front of Mr. Taffle as he ran.

"Mr. Manley, I'm in big trouble! There is a group of crazy duplicate clones after me, and there's a noseless man who thinks he's a honey badger who's also after me! Also, my ex-girlfriend has been kidnapped!" gasped Mr. Taffle. He immediately realized he had just called her his *ex*-girlfriend. He found this interesting.

"Loosey Goosey Level 7.2," yawned Mr. Manley as he calmly blew his pinwheel. "Where are you?"

"I'm currently running back to a bar called The Truth. But I'm not sure exactly where it is. There's a mannequin lying in a nearby alleyway that may have the answer to who kidnapped her."

"Well, looky who ended up in Very, Very, Very, Very, Very Funkytown. I'm shocked you were granted the password. That's not too far from my The Tree House. Scan the horizon and look for me."

"Look for you?" wondered Mr. Taffle aloud. Mr. Manley's projection was already doing a preemptive Projecto hard smack to Mr. Taffle's face while exhaling a big breath of, "Youheardmeyou heardmeyouheardmeyouheardme."

Mr. Taffle scanned the horizon and spotted something blinking in the distance. It was a 30-foot neon sign depicting Mr. Manley holding two bikini-clad women—one under each arm—making it rain hundred-dollar bills.

"Just head for the neon sign that's a representation of the dark side of vulture capitalism, and you'll find The Truth," explained Mr. Manley. "I'll meet you there, and I'll bring you a diet soda of my computer's choosing." Mr. Manley's Projection once again blew his pinwheel, and then disappeared.

Only moments later, Mr. Taffle heard the roar of the Winnebago's engine as it quickly gained on him from the bottom of the hill. Jack Honey Badger, with the ceremonial hair clippers lodged in his forehead, clung onto the Winnebago's hood for dear life.

Mr. Taffle actually took a moment to note how surprised he was that the animal vs. animal showdown had turned in the hyenas' favor. Mr. Taffle turned back around just in time to see a 50-foot Viking warship on semi-truck wheels cut directly in front of him.

He spun wildly off the road, tripped, and smashed his head hard on the ground. The Winnebago slammed on its brakes, which consequently shot Jack Honey Badger, like a cannonball, smashing through the hull of the Viking ship.

Mr. Taffle watched from his position upside-down on the ground an army of one-foot-tall Vikings, wearing horned helmets and armed with mini swords and battle axes, charge out of the ship to attack the Winnebago. Mr. Taffle wobbled to his feet for two seconds, and then passed out cold.

Chapter Twelve

The Fascinating History of the Fun-Sized Norse Warriors

he entire history of the Fun-sized Norse Warriors was also written on a scroll from 1040 AD, proving Banzan Kubo was indeed on to something with his important document/scroll theory. However, the Norse Scroll Master had bafflingly sloppy penmanship, especially while scrolling at sea, and the runic alphabet was not only extremely hard to read, but gave the linguistic expert in charge of translating the scroll a serious migraine. Therefore, only the highlights had been translated and then funneled through the voice of cultural clichés and stereotypes.

Oh, my dear Solveig. How I miss thee. May the gods bless you as well as Sigrid, Frigg, Sif, Astrid, Ingrid, and Freya. I must admit I don't miss Gunhild at al. In fact, I think it would be best if you sacrificed her to Odin before I return, if that's cool. That is, if we do return from the sea.

We find ourselves in a bit of a snafu because Knut acted like a nut while celebrating his newly snagged feudal overlordship in northern France. After inhaling the smoke from an enchanted plant he scored in Constantinople, he decided it would be a good idea to paint "Big Daddy Duchy" on the ship's sail in walrus blood. All I said was, "Perhaps if you would have put out the torch first, then maybe you wouldn't have burned down the sail of the ship," but he lost his wits like the God Tyr losing his right hand while binding the great wolf Fenir. I was forced to defend myself from the mighty blade of the battle-axe he had stolen from an impish baron in the Carolingian Empire. Anyway, now he's up in Valhalla, and so are Arne, Ulf, Birger, Torsten, Gorm, Sven, Halfdan, and Leif, who all fought bravely by his side. So, now we are missing not only our sail, but many of our best rowers as well. And I'm afraid that perhaps ditching our emergency provisions in order to make room for those 200 sparkly crucifixes was not a wise decision. Oh, my dear Solvieg, how I should have listened to your prophecy when you foretold that 200 sparkly crucifixes would be the final straw in our assimilation into Christendom. And I haven't even gotten to the part about how we're being followed by a silver ship flying through the sky. Everyone thinks this is Freya, but I say no way, since it's no secret that her chariot is always being pulled by flying cats. And invisible flying cats are just a silly child's myth.

Oh, my dear Solvieg, how I miss thee. Well, it turns out the flying chariot was indeed a ship forged from magical metals and flown by these lizard people that actually have a lot more in common with birds and are surprisingly cute. They come from an exact duplicate planet as our own, only on the opposite side of the goddess Sunna. Turns out, billions of years ago their ancestors lived on our planet too, only as giant monster versions *of the lizard people that weren't cute at all and were called by the name "dinosaur." However, one day Thor got pissed at the goddess Iounn for hoarding all of her applesauce and, in a drunken rage, he smashed a colossal rock with his mighty hammer, causing a chunk to crash to our planet, killing off their ancestral beasts. However, since they were on an exact duplicate planet as ours, their dinosaurs didn't die; they proceeded to partake in this hocus-pocus thingy called "evolution" for millions of years. Thus, the reason they're now so smart and so cute. The reason I know this, my dear Solvieg, is because our entire ship was taken into their flying chariot, and we are now their prisoners. Oh, the unspeakable things they make us do. And, for some unknown reason, they have removed all our baby toes. I mean, while it is true that baby toes don't really have a purpose, it's just still so unexplainably creepy! The cute lizard leader can communicate telepathically with me and does so every time they stick this precious metal probe up my bottom hole. Her name is Lunchee, and she's addicted to this substance called Paffa that she squirts into her ears, eyes, and bottom hole. This magic elixir makes her constantly blab about all kinds of bizarre-ass stuff. In fact, sometimes she forgets to breathe and passes out. It also makes her racist, as displayed by her disparaging remarks towards a pink and blue salamander-like creature named Beeboo, who secretly brings us pineapple snacks. Lunchee's life story was as interesting as it was scandalous, and I really appreciated how her chapter of nepotism and sadomasochism tied together in such an unexpected way. But sprinkled in with these all-night Paffa confessions were key clues I gathered in hopes we could plan our escape, Odin willing. Turns out, there were escape chariots on the ship that could be controlled simply by the mind, which would work as long as the probes remained in our bottom holes. This would also give us access to the shrinking technique, which would allow us to shrink to a size small enough to squeeze through the cage bars of the Maze of Pain in which we're forced to race against each other at the end of every week.*

Oh, my dear Solvieg, I'm worried you may never have the opportunity to read this scroll, as Lunchee never properly explained this thingy called the space-time continuum. Now, instead of going home in the present time, we are back to Earth in the future. And the probes up our bottom holes ran out of batteries. So now we remain on average one foot one inches tall. And in this futuristic society, everyone hates little people. Even the little people hate us. That's more messed up than the fact that The Tree of Life is guarded by an unreliable squirrel that loves hatred. And, oh, poor, poor Gudrum! He was stomped by this barbaric elderly man's walking cane while the wrinkled bastard sang this famous futuristic hymn, "Short people got no reason to live."

I'm afraid there is no place for us in this futuristic dystopian nightmare. We have been forced to hide underground in a series of waterways called the sewer, which smell worse than Bjorn's dungeon after a holiday weekend, and I'm not exaggerating. We make nightly raids into the castles of these futuristic sad sacks of dung and steal their provisions, preferably the meat in cans because then we can store them without spoiling, which is nice. I fear we will never be accepted anywhere in the future, so I will most likely be seeing you in Valhalla very soon.

Oh, my dear Solvieg! There has been a recent development that makes me have some hope for a future here in the future. Magnus the Good stole a treasure trove of this funky canned meat called Spam (which I believe is made up entirely of lips and bottom holes) from a contortionist named Saucy Susan. Magnus the Good overheard Saucy Susan talking, between her legs in a pretzel position, to a long-bearded gypsy named Niles (who hung bricks from his nipples and genitals) regarding a hidden world that welcomes the freakiest of the freaks. That is, if you are proven worthy, upon arrival a mystical woman with a short temper called the Duchess will grant you the secret password. Perhaps we will take a journey there, and perhaps will be granted the secret password willingly... or by force. And then we will raid their lands and take power. I'll let you know how it all went and stuff. Give my love to Sigrid, Frigg, Sif, Astrid, Ingrid, and Freya. Gunhild better be dead now, or I'm going to be seriously pissed.

Chapter Thirteen

The Dangerous Labyrinth Of Pineapples

Mr. Taffle slowly drifted back into consciousness to find that he was now strapped onto a surgical table. The very first thing he thought is that he hoped his pants were okay. Yes, they were still on, undamaged, and still looked so damn good on him. He wasn't sure if he was more freaked out about being strapped to the table or the fact that he kept thinking about the well-being of his pants. He soon realized he was surrounded by one-foot one-inch-tall Viking surgeons dressed in full surgical attire, but with war helmets and Ragnar Lothbrok replica boots. There was even a group of tiny Viking surgeons looking down from an observation room behind plate glass. The tiny Viking surgeons didn't notice when Mr. Taffle regained consciousness and continued to chatter among themselves.

"Somebody really needs to manufacture leather pants for little people," said Halfdan Ragnarsson,

"Yeah, there's a huge market for that," snickered Magnus the Good.

"Honestly, I don't care too much for your sarcasm," replied Halfdan Ragnarsson.

"You'd have a better chance at creating a leather pant clothing line for toddlers," said Snorri Sturluson.

"Moving on," huffed Halfdan Ragnarsson. "I'm going to pitch the idea to those loaded little people from the Union of Myanmar."

"They actually prefer you refer to them as the dwarves from Burma," corrected Wayland the Smith.

"Quit flapping the jaw and get ready to saw," sighed Egil Skallagrimsson as he turned on a mini-surgical saw.

"What in the hell are you doing?!" screamed Mr. Taffle as he desperately tried to break free.

"Oh, look who decided to wake up just in time to go back to sleep," chuckled Harald Fairhair diabolically, as she covered Mr. Taffle's mouth with an inhaler of anesthesia.

Mr. Taffle once again slowly awakened, but this time he found himself in the middle of an indoor maze made up entirely of pineapples. The maze stretched for miles. Once again, his first thought was about the safety of his pants. Also, once again, there was a pack of the tiny Vikings armed with lances and battle-axes who charged out of a pineapple-shaped door. The smallest one of them was only 10 inches tall, but wore a helmet with a bear head that made him look two feet tall. The weight of his helmet made it difficult for him to hold his head up. This was Bjakre the Bear.

"Greeting, Sword Guy. My name is Bjakre the Bear. Honestly, it's really just Bjakre, but I thought I should include the Bear add-on in English, or you might not get that I'm fierce as a bear. Do you agree?" asked Bjakre the Bear.

"I mean, the bear head on your head is a solid clue you want to be a bear. Now, I'm afraid I must be going," said Mr. Taffle as he stood up, only to be immediately knocked back down by a foot sweep from Egil Skallagrimsson's iron lance. The lance was decorated with magnificent leafy foliage carvings.

"We know that you must be a very close associate of the Farmer Ted 8s, as they call you Sword Guy. You would only call someone by a nickname if they meant something to you, do you agree?" asked Bjakre the Bear.

"I mean, technically, that would be a good assumption but—"

"TELL US WHERE THE UNDERGROUND FARM OF THE TWO-UDDER COWS IS LOCATED!" demanded Bjakre the Bear.

"I have no idea. Honestly, I just met them. They were helping me find my girlfriend, who is in trouble. And that's why I need to GO RIGHT NOW, PLEASE!"

Once again, Mr. Taffle had called her his girlfriend, but he decided not to correct himself. Magnus the Good slammed his war hammer on the ground, which shattered its serpent war hammer ring wrap into pieces. Tension in the air was thick.

"The cycle of abuse is a social cycle theory that explains patterns of behavior in an abusive relationship," calmly explained Bjakre the Bear. "It was important for me to understand this theory so I could intellectualize why I was so compelled to recreate the exact maze—comprised solely of pineapples—that our cute lizard captors had forced us to race in at the end of every week. However, the cute lizards were way more technologically advanced than humans, with their mazes having these totally trippy dimensional portals that let you jump in and reappear in another part of the maze, and lots of other futuristic bells and whistles. But that wouldn't be realistic to try to recreate, so instead, we have crafted a three-mile labyrinth with lots of hidden, creative surprises that will kill you, chop off a limb, burn your skin off, and other cool stuff like that."

"Well, I can relate to you in regards to working very hard, and this maze must have taken quite a bit of very hard work to build," said Mr. Taffle, digging hard into his sales manipulation techniques.

"Yes, it was quite a major operation, but we made it happen with the help of the entire community, since, at the time of construction, they still feared us. That was, until your associates, the Farmer Ted 8s, started calling us the "Fun-sized Norse Warriors." Then nobody took us seriously, and now," he became slightly emotional. "I'm forgetting my point. Do you agree?"

"I think you were going to tie in how this labyrinth of pineapples comes into play," said Mr. Taffle.

"Oh, clever Sword Guy. Let us not forget Loki became a mare because he really liked horses."

"I have no idea what that means."

"Tell us EVERTHING or you're going to have to try and find your way out of the Dangerous Labyrinth of Pineapples. You know that's not going to be likely, as I'm pretty certain the only thing Odin likes about you is your stunning pants."

"The only thing I really know about the Farmer Ted 8s is that the interior of their Winnebago has a Japanese theme that really crosses the line of cultural appropriation, and that it transforms into a movie theater."

Suddenly, horrified shrieks coming from Halfdan Ragnarsson's walkie-talkie interrupted, "THE FARMER TED 8S HAVE BREACHED THE COMPOUND!" The Vikings urgently charged back through the entrance. Mr. Taffle quickly followed, but the pineapple door was slammed in his face and firmly locked from behind.

Mr. Taffle would have to make it through the Dangerous Labyrinth of Pineapples if he was to have any chance of getting out. Or... he could just climb on top and over the maze. The Fun-sized Norse Warriors had constructed the labyrinth to the size specifications of someone one-foot one-inch tall. That meant that the pineapple walls were only six feet high, which was pretty easy for Mr. Taffle to climb over. This meant that he wouldn't have to find his way through the maze at all. In fact, if he stood on top of each of the pineapple walls, he could spot most of the traps from above and avoid them. Even so, he almost stepped on a glossy portion of the floor that turned out to be a glue trap. But just as he was about to step down into the glue, the pants wouldn't let him. He said, "Thank you, pants," to the pants before he could stop himself.

It took 14 minutes for Mr. Taffle to cut across the maze and reach the "Exit" sign (written in pineapples) over a pineapple-shaped tube. He could barely squeeze through the tube, which was made up of a kaleidoscope of pineapples. It seemed like every color that ever existed was represented and, due to the cramped space, he got a slight kink in his neck trying to check out the awe-inspiring pineapple psychedelia. At the end of the kaleidoscope, there was another pineapple door that resembled an over-wing exit on a passenger plane, with a pineapple parachute backpack leaning up against it. It was obvious what this meant. They must be high enough up that Mr. Taffle would have to parachute out of there. He had read stories about how, in the 1970s, planes would get hijacked by robbers who would then parachute out of the plane with the ransom money. One lunatic who had never even parachuted out of a plane before took part and successfully landed on the ground. So at least there was a small sample size. He repeated "so at least there was a small sample size" 15 times in row before he finally strapped on the pine-apple parachute pack. When he opened the door, he found he was, in fact, just on top of the tallest building on the street. That wasn't such a big deal, as the building was only nine feet tall. He took off the pineapple parachute pack and left it for the next person to be unnecessarily terrified.

Mr. Taffle leapt off the building, bouncing off a mini-willow tree and crushing a handcrafted mini-horse-drawn carriage into pieces. Everything on the entire block had been modeled after the Viking's home fishing village Kaupang, scaled down to give the illusion they were at their original size before they were shrunk. So it was easy for Mr. Taffle to spot the out-of-place mini golf cart parked between two miniature war ponies wearing posh plate armor.

CHAPTER FOURTEEN

Piss Piss Piss

r. Taffle floored the golf cart to its maximum speed of 15 miles per hour as he sped away from the miniaturized fishing village. He was relieved when he finally turned a corner and found himself back in the menacing concrete jungle of downtown. And when he located the neon sign of Mr. Manley's representation of the dark side of vulture capitalism, he was giddy.

He drove down the alley where he had last seen Monique the Mannequin, but she wasn't there anymore. The one clue that could help him find The Mannequin Madam was gone. He was devastated.

His car was also gone, most likely being driven around by a man who thought he was a honey badger. Oh, well.

"Yo, Taffle comma Mr.!" It was Mr. Manley. He had waited for Mr. Taffle by the wall of The Truth, but The Wall wasn't in sight—unless, of course, he was blending in with the actual wall. Mr. Manley was still wearing the swimming attire, but he'd taken it to another level with a full-body camouflaged spear-fishing wetsuit. He held his pinwheel in one hand and a can of soda in the other. A zebra-print lamp was clenched between his legs.

"Nice night to hit some birdies," Mr. Manley smirked as Mr. Taffle drove up in the mini-golf cart.

"Excuse me?"

"Perfect evening to putt on some greens," replied Mr. Manley with even a bigger smirk.

"Huh?"

"People driving golf carts are sometimes playing golf according to *Golf Digest*."

"What? Sorry, I'm still a bit disoriented from the anesthesia given to me by the Fun-sized Norse Warriors before they performed surgery on me."

"That's pretty strange. Here's your diet soda," said Mr. Manley, as he handed Mr. Taffle a diet cream soda. He then blew his pinwheel.

"Did you look for the mannequin?"

"I didn't find a mannequin, but I did find this really funky vintage lamp. And here comes a gang of clones riding Vespas armed with tasers," he said matter-of-factly as the Farmer Ted 8s quickly surrounded them on hot pink motor scooters. "I'm going to take a wild guess these are the clones after you,"

"Yes."

"And I'm probably now also in danger."

"Yes."

"For the 57th time, I don't want to buy this damn pinwheel or any Chiclets!" screamed Mr. Manley, as he chucked his pinwheel into Mr. Taffle's face. He then put the lamp on the top of his head and slowly backed up.

"I would hate to have to rescind his pool privileges!"

"The cabana boys will be pissed!"

"There'll be no fresh towels!"

"He just might not be exclusive pool club material after all!" said Farmer Ted 5, perfectly imitating Thurston Howell III, the millionaire from *Gilligan's Island*. "I'll call Barb and have her check his current membership status!"

"I got Barb on the line!" said Farmer Ted 4, as he passed an invisible phone to Farmer Ted 5.

"Barb says he should die, but his mustache should live!"

Mr. Manley stopped, skipped in a complete circle three times, and then continued right back to the group. "Tell Barb I can hang at the club. *No problemo.* That's Spanish."

All the Farmer Ted 8s golf clapped at the same time.

"Sword guy, on the other hand..."

"Needs to have his membership canceled permanently."

"No need to bother Barb again."

"You're a Barb botherer."

"I am a Barb botherer," realized Farmer Ted 5.

The Farmer Ted 8s pointed their tasers at Mr. Taffle just as the red and blue lights of a cop car drove towards them.

"Nobody told me it was lucky Sword Guy day."

"A clerical error."

"Call Barb and have her fire herself."

And on that... the Farmer Ted 8s drove off.

"And considering what a blabbermouth the local sheriff's cunning wife is, I better skedaddle as well," said Mr. Manley.

"Well, I need to stay, find that mannequin, and tell the police about what happened."

"Good move. I'll be back at The Tree House bonding with my new lamp if you need anything else and are willing to deposit more non-traceable currency. Good times, Mr. Taffle. See you mañana. Again, that's Spanish." Mr. Manley blew his pinwheel, picked up the lamp, and hopscotched away.

Police Officer Emme Pulous approached Mr. Taffle with her gun drawn. She had transferred to this precinct over six months ago, and everything just kept getting stranger and stranger. Why was this zone in the middle of downtown off limits to police officers? Who was this Duchess she kept hearing rumors about? She couldn't get a straight answer out of anyone. Literally everyone she brought this up with would change the subject. Even when she pressed her own partner, he would instantaneously spin into a diatribe about "the sociological impact of the symbiotic relationship between police officers and the donut in modern American culture" for hours. The real reason for all this strangeness was a mix-up in paperwork at the precinct. On the day Officer Pulous had been scheduled for her precinct's mandatory hypnosis session, she had accidentally ordered a variety of five large pizzas instead. This glitch in the scheduling software was a one-time occurrence. It was the mayor himself who had made it mandatory for every police officer to be hypnotized after he himself had been hypnotized by the governor, who in turn had been hypnotized by someone called the Duchess.

About five months into this conundrum, Officer Pulous' hands started to shake whenever she felt like shooting someone... which was anytime she wasn't asleep. A few days later, she secretly started referring to herself as Mama Medicine and started taking the law into her own hands by cruising Very, Very, Very, Very, Very Funkytown on her off hours.

"HANDS UP!" ordered Mama Medicine, as she shined her flash-light in Mr. Taffle's face.

"No, it's okay. I was about to call you guys. I have information about a woman who was abducted from a night club tonight and whose life I believe is in danger."

"What night club?"

"The Truth," said Mr. Taffle as he pointed to the giant question mark on the wall. "There's a hidden passage behind that question mark. You can't enter unless you give The Wall—not the actual wall, but a guy in body paint that makes him blend in with the wall amazingly well—the secret password. He might even be here; it's really hard to tell. He's the one who possesses the remote control that moves the question mark into the brick wall. But I can clear this all up if I can just find her mannequin."

"I've had some reports tonight about a man called Sword Guy in this area intimidating people with a sword. Do you know anything about that?"

Mr. Taffle wrestled internally about whether lying in this case could be classified as a white lie, beneficial to both parties. He pinched his left nipple. Even though Mama Medicine wasn't privy to The Taffle Tells, she knew this nervous tic must mean that he knew something about this Sword Guy. At that moment, Mama Medicine's flashlight located the sword Mr. Taffle had ditched on the ground earlier.

"That's not my sword, but was stolen from the Museum of Swords that's located in the bar. I promise you I can explain everything."

Mama Medicine promptly grabbed Mr. Taffle by his hair and shoved his face onto the sidewalk.

"This is a giant mistake!" he screamed in a muffled voice. It came out sounding like, "I'm a violent fake!"

He somehow managed to pry his face off the concrete just enough to spot Monique hanging out of a dumpster in the alley.

"THAT'S HER MANNEQUIN!'"

Mama Medicine wasn't going to fall for the ol' mannequin-in-the-dumpster trick, even though she knew there was no such trick… *but there should be, DAMMIT.* She pulled out her handcuffs and was about to arrest him on suspicion of intimidation with a dangerous weapon. And yes, she was going to tell headquarters she arrested him in this part of downtown. And she didn't care if they would again try to change the subject into a spirited debate on whether cauliflower is really just albino broccoli. *IT ISN'T!*

Just as she was about to put him in handcuffs, Mr. Taffle delivered a hard back-kick to her head. Considering that Mr. Taffle couldn't normally even touch his toes, the most plausible explanation was that his pants were the ones that caused this incredibly flexible kick.

"I'M SO SORRY! I SWEAR MY PANTS DID THAT!" Mr. Taffle called back as he sprinted over to Monique and scooped her up.

So, this was it. Mama Medicine, despite her recent addiction to hoarding guns, had never shot her gun at anyone in her entire three years as a police officer. But now, she was going to kill this man. And frankly, it felt nice.

"You're the poison and Mama Medicine is the antidote!" she shrieked as she fired her gun at Mr. Taffle.

Thankfully, her shaking-hands problem made her miss by three feet, and she ended up shooting a trashcan instead. As Mr. Taffle tossed Monique over the alley fence, she fired at him again. This time, she missed so poorly, she shot 50 yards into a sewer drain. Mr. Taffle quickly climbed up the fence and disappeared over the other side before she could get off another shot.

The moment he landed on the other side of the fence, he looked up and screamed. "ALPACAAAAAHHHH!" The escaped rabid Disco Ball Alpaca charged at him from down the street. He quickly sprinted over to the next fence straight ahead of them and tossed Monique over. As he struggled to pull himself over, the Disco Ball Alpaca lunged at his pants. While failing to bite Mr. Taffle, the alpaca did manage to send a spiral of spit that somehow navigated like a heat-seeking missile to Mr. Taffle's face. Unexpectedly, he wasn't upset at getting drenched in a preposterous amount of alpaca spit. He had never heard of an alpaca exhibiting this kind of violent behavior before. The only logical explanation was this had been caused by the abuse of being kept in a cage dressed as a disco ball.

"Run free, Disco Ball Alpaca! The world is yours!"

Mr. Taffle scooped up Monique and dashed out into the street without looking. A golden 1973 Citroen Dsuper5-Convertible, aka a hip French car with an even hipper mural of Serge Gainsbourg painted on the hood, slammed on its brakes to avoid running over Mr. Taffle. It was Le Rat, dressed in a gold and black velour astrology-themed kimono cardigan.

"My girlfriend has been kidnapped! You've got to help me!" pleaded Mr. Taffle, again not correcting himself when calling her his girlfriend.

"I told you not to buy the Pants of Insanity! Now you are on your own!" Le Rat hit the gas, peeled off, and then once again slammed on the brakes. "PISS, PISS, PISS!"

He hit reverse and returned to Mr. Taffle. "First, you must agree to take off the pants immediately."

"I will, but—

"But what?!"

"I don't have any underwear on," admitted Mr. Taffle reluctantly, as an invisible dull jackknife gutted out whatever pride he'd had left.

"PISS, PISS, PISS!" Le Rat slammed his head against the steering wheel for each "Piss." "Get in, Taffle, and leave that mannequin!"

"Sorry, it's my girlfriend's mannequin, so she's coming with me," said Mr. Taffle as he hopped in with Monique under his arm, again not correcting himself for calling her his girlfriend.

"PISS, PISS, PISS!" Le Rat said as he slammed his head against the back of his Serge Gainsbourg head pillow. Then he peeled out.

"What size are you?" Le Rat asked as they charged through the door of the Keytar Clothing and Pipe Shop.

"I'm a...pretty close to a 30-inch waist I think and a 34-inch, you know, leg."

"INSEAM, TAFFLE!" screamed Le Rat as he rushed toward a rack featuring a wide assortment of pants. He maniacally went through the entire rack, leaving each pair of pants on the floor as he inspected them. "THE ONE SIZE I DON'T HAVE! OH, WAIT! WE JUST RECEIVED A NEW SHIPMENT TODAY, YAY!"

Le Rat quickly disappeared into the back of the store. Mr. Taffle took this opportunity to unzip the hidden pouch in Monique's unitard. He pulled out a folded piece of paper that read in The Mannequin Madam's rushed penmanship, "The Random Hallway—17659 Kilm Street."

Le Rat quickly returned with a large, unopened box of pants and set it on the ground. He pulled out from underneath his kimono a rare medieval anelace dagger from 14th century England. In reality, it was a replica he had bought from the Museum of Swords gift shop. Le Rat raised the dagger dramatically and stabbed it into the packing tape on the box of pants.

"Where's Kilm Street?" asked Mr. Taffle nonchalantly.

"Just three blocks south of here," Le Rat said as he excitedly yanked out from the box a pair of jeans with slight bell-bottoms.

"Yes! I found your size! Yes!"

"I'm sorry, but I don't have time," said Mr. Taffle. He grabbed Monique and headed for the exit. Le Rat blocked his path, unintentionally holding the dagger in a menacing way. "You have forced my hand! I will tell you what I swore I would never tell anyone besides my relentlessly nosey plumber Phil."

Le Rat now held the dagger only an inch away from Mr. Taffle's Adam's apple.

"Five months and four days ago, I received a shipment of forty pairs of leather pants. And it was four months and 27 days ago when a customer who tried on a pair of leather pants from that shipment...started to glow. Soon, more people who tried on the leather pants glowed, just as you are now glowing."

"You think I'm glowing?"

"I don't THINK, Taffle, I KNOW you're currently encircled in a dark pastel green glow. But why do some people glow and why do some not glow? I asked myself that for weeks. And then for two months and one week, I did intense research and surveillance on anyone who glowed from wearing the leather pants. And then for half a month, I thought I knew the reason they glowed. But then for just under a month, I denied it all. And now, for most of last month and all this month, I've accepted what I now know to be 100% true: I have no idea. But I do know what happens when the people who glow wear these leather pants."

Mr. Taffle didn't care; he just wanted to get the hell out of there. But he knew he wasn't going to be allowed to go until Le Rat finished his explanation. "What happens?"

Le Rat milked this moment by intensely squinting his eyes in that now-familiar spaghetti western showdown style before finally whispering, "Artistic Treachery."

"What does that mean?"

"You're going to be killed in a way that will involve creative technical proficiency, beauty, and emotional power!"

Mr. Taffle quickly opened the door to leave. But before he could go, Le Rat slammed the door shut, leaving some of Mr. Taffle's hair jammed in the door.

"So, I'm just going to take a wild stab that the pants JUST HAPPENED to lead you straight to Very, Very, Very, Very, Very Funkytown. And then you JUST HAPPENED to constantly run into the freakiest of freaks, as if you were a disco light to a funky firefly?"

"Oh you mean like I just happened to run into you," said Mr. Taffle with an awkward wink that looked like a mosquito had just flown into his eyeball.

"Nice burn, Taffle!" said Le Rat with genuine surprise.

And then, as if on cue, security strobe lights flickered throughout the shop. Le Rat vaulted over the front counter to check the security camera monitors. They showed six different angles of the street below. And on each screen was a member of the Farmer Ted 8s. "Please tell me you haven't met six men who have the haircut of the Earth with the moon rotating around it and the North Star in the distance?"

"What? *That's* what it is?! Well, I got that completely wrong, as usual," sighed Mr. Taffle, feeling the familiar losing sting he got each night while watching *Jeopardy*.

"NO! GOD, NO! FOR THE LOVE OF GOD! NO, GOD! THERE CAN'T BE!"

Le Rat leaped back over the counter and sprinted towards the changing rooms.

"Where are you going?!"

"Changing room number 4!"

On the keytar-shaped bench of Changing Room 4 were two seat belts with keytar-shaped buckles. "Buckle up tight and leave the mannequin!" ordered Le Rat.

"No, sir! I'm bringing this mannequin back to The Mannequin Madam! And I'm not going to repeat myself about that again!"

"I recommend from now on that you do everything the opposite of what you would normally do. That is your only chance." Le Rat held out the keytar-shaped silver ring on his middle finger and waved it in a figure-eight pattern. Mr. Taffle buckled his seat belt just as the entire bench flipped and they disappeared into the wall, with the bench being replaced by an identical keytar bench.

The keytar bench flew through the cavern like an out-of-control ski lift. Laser beams shooting out from the bottom of the bench projected glowing keytars on the cave walls.

"I can't believe I forgot your replacement jeans! You're totally Taffled!" shouted Le Rat, unsure of why he just used Mr. Taffle's last name as an adjective.

"I am not Taffled! I must and will save her."

"Each person who has glowed has suffered the same fate. They always end up in Very, Very, Very, Very, Very Funkytown. A place they were never meant to be. That's how I know the tragic fates of 16 of the 17 people who have glowed."

"What about the 17th person?"

"Geeeeeeeeeeee, I wonder who that could be? Unfortunately, there is only one way out of here. We have to go through..." Le Rat knew he really had to lay it on thick that what he was about to say was a big deal. So instead of giving Mr. Taffle the usual spaghetti-western squint, he bugged his eyes out. This inadvertently caused some nostril rotation, "The... Dinner... Party."

"Seems a little late to be having a dinner party," zinged Mr. Taffle, trying to ignore the nostril rotation.

"It's always time for a dinner party at the Dinner Party," zinged back Le Rat as he began to spin his legs in a running motion. "Unbuckle now!"

The bench didn't slow down as they sped up to the exit ramp. Le Rat unbuckled and ran off gracefully, like a man that had done it many times before. Mr. Taffle barely got his buckle off and tumbled hard to the ground. And so did Monique. Le Rat deliberately hadn't warned Mr. Taffle about how to dismount properly, as seeing him lying down in minor pain was another way to mine anything positive from the screwed-up situation he found himself in yet again.

"There are the four *No Matter Whats* regarding the Dinner Party," announced Le Rat, standing over Mr. Taffle. "Always keep a smile on your face NO MATTER WHAT, keep walking forward NO MATTER WHAT, don't look anyone in the eye NO MATTER WHAT, and never say anything to anyone about anything NO MATTER WHAT."

"Okay, I understand, sir. But if there is anything supernatural about these pants, it's that they're trying to protect me."

"They're not protecting you. They just wanted to make sure they have some fun before their new toy is broken. Like an orca playing toss Sammy the Smiling Seal and then toss Sammy the Smiling Seal again and then toss Sammy the Smiling Seal again and then toss Sammy the Smiling Seal again and then rip Sammy the Smiling Seal's flesh apart while Sammy the Smiling Seal is crying for his mommy!"

"I'M NOT GOING TO CRY TO MY MOMMY! I HAVE TO SAVE THE MANNEQUIN MADAM! I LOVE HER, DAMMIT! SO SHUT

UP!" Mr. Taffle had completely lost his fear of being punched in the face.

"Look, I have the deepest respect for the institution of love. However, the last time I was at the Dinner Party, I was tricked into having the endless salad bar and didn't escape for four months and nine days. Now, just imagine what could happen to you while you're wearing the Pants of Insanity." Le Rat walked over to a chain link ladder and climbed up 10 feet until he reached a hatch on the roof. "Here we go again," he sighed as he opened the hatch and climbed inside.

Chapter Fifteen

The Dinner Party

Le Rat's prominent influence in Very, Very, Very, Very, Very Funkytown was cemented on the day he challenged Genghis Khan to drag race their souped-up Pocket Rockets through the center of town. Genghis Khan's Honda Civic lost control, smashed into a low-flying blimp (shaped like a bus bench with an advertisement for the Law Office of "Justice" Jerry Curl and Associates), and burst into a fireball. This caused Genghis Khan's artificial skin to completely burn off and reveal his true robot face, which ended the debate about whether he was, in fact, a simulacrum. So, when Le Rat requested one of the Dinner Party employee lockers, this was given to him with no question. And if anyone suspected he might use it as a secret entrance into the Dinner Party, nobody cared enough to bring it up.

Le Rat, Mr. Taffle, and Monique exited out of employee locker #4349 undetected, as, thankfully, the evening shift had started only an hour earlier. This employee locker room was as massive as a basketball arena. Just how many employees could have possibly worked at the Dinner Party?

9,563 full-time and 659 part-time workers.

As they approached the swinging kitchen door labeled "The Dinner Party," which led out to the Dinner Party, Le Rat clutched Mr. Taffle's shoulder and looked him dead in the eye. "I swear on the souls of St. Paol Aoerliann, St. Tudwal, St. Brieg, St Malou and even St. Samsun of Dol, that you will have a way better chance of making it through the Dinner Party if you take off the pants. And, yes, if that means you will be wearing just your birthday suit, then so be it."

Surprisingly, for some reason Mr. Taffle actually believed him. "Yeah... but... still, no way in hell."

"Here we go again," sighed Le Rat. Then he swung the door open.

The Dinner Party was an endless sea of sheer extravagant over-indulgence—26.2188 miles of it, to be exact. This specific length had been decided so that they could use the tagline: "It's literally a marathon of gluttony!" Men in formal suits and women in ball gowns wandered about like busy ants, eating mounds of hors d'oeuvres and drinking from wine glasses the size of fishbowls. However, if one looked at the guests closely, one could see that they were actually ragged-looking, as though they hadn't showered in weeks—because they hadn't left in weeks. The stench of perfume, cologne, and horrible B.O combined had the same effects as the MSG flavor enhancer in Chinese food. If one were allergic to the smell, it could cause nausea, vomiting, cramps, diarrhea, gas, heartburn, and headaches.

"Remember, look straight ahead with a relaxed smile," Le Rat said with a smile that made him look as if he were going to throw up at any moment.

They had walked only 20 feet into the party when Mr. Taffle dared to peek out at some of this vulgar display of excess. He couldn't help but stare at a Statue of Liberty-sized head of opera legend Luciano Pavarotti in the distance being overtaken by a team of filthy coal miners prying out chunks of lasagna from his beard with pickaxes.

Then Mr. Taffle, for the briefest of moments, caught the eye of a Salvador Dali wannabe sporting a 10-foot version of his famous handlebar mustache. Ironically, the Salvador Dali wannabe claimed he was the real simulacrum of Salvador Dali, when, in actuality, he was Robert Wexler from East Rockaway, New York.

"Thank you for admiring my amazing mustache!" announced Salvador Dali proudly, as he trailed behind them with a psychotic grin on his face.

Le Rat quickly jumped between them as if he was ready for this to happen. "So sorry! But we're late for spearmint Tar Tars with Yasha and Sasha!"

"That sounds delightfully grand. I think I'll tag along!" celebrated Salvador Dali. He managed to dodge around Le Rat and get back to Mr. Taffle. "Your pants are like a forgotten poem found at the bottom of a well!"

"Thank you," replied Mr. Taffle. Le Rat's expression advertised loud and clear that Mr. Taffle's life was now in danger.

"YASHA AND SASHA WOULD NEVER ALLOW YOUR MUSTACHE!" Le Rat shrieked desperately. "YOU'D HAVE TO SHAVE IT OFF IN ORDER TO ATTEND!"

"NEVEEEEEEEEEEER!" shouted back an offended Salvador Dali, as he tried to spit a loogie down to Le Rat's feet—though it mostly got caught on the right tip of his mustache. He stormed off. Le Rat closed his eyes and took the kind of deep, calming breath a person takes when they know they have just avoided death.

"Stare straight ahead at ALL TIMES and don't Taffle again," scolded Le Rat, not realizing he had just used "Taffle" as a verb.

They had embarked on quite the trek. While the sped-up ballroom dancing music played from secret speakers planted throughout the Dinner Party did help keep them moving, soon they were both exhausted and drenched in sweat. Mr. Taffle grabbed Monique's glitter unitard and patted down his face, which made him look like he might be acting inappropriately with the mannequin.

"WHAT IN THE WORLD ARE YOU DOING TO THAT MANNEQUIN?!" shouted a gigantic woman off to his right. Mr. Taffle accidentally glanced in her direction. There were 20 other enormous guests at her table, each looking as if they had swallowed 20 other guests from the empty table next to them—which they had actually done three days earlier.

The guests, including the men, each had caked on more layers of makeup than a professional circus clown. They had all applied fake birthmarks to their cheeks, which looked like puddles of chocolate or poop needing to be wiped off. They all wore colonial wigs spray-painted with pastel colors to match their colonial gowns. But only one of these guests, in addition to being draped in hip-hop bling, wore her tricorn hat sideways.

This was the one and only Duchess of Very, Very, Very, Very, Very Funkytown, and this was her table. The Duchess pulled out a switchblade that shot out a golden spork with sharp, curved tines. The spork hooked onto Mr. Taffle's shirt and yanked him over until he was face-to-face with her massive face. It had been so quick that Le Rat hadn't even seen it happen.

"Do you have a license for that mannequin?" she inquired.

"Um, why would I need a license for a mannequin?"

"Well, you don't, but since I'm the Duchess of Very, Very, Very, Very, Very Funkytown, I think you should definitely have to have one!" she declared as she jerked Monique out of his arms and into her lap.

"What is the name of this man who dares to bring an unlicensed mannequin to the Dinner Party?"

"Mr.—" is all he said before he was cut off.

"MR.?! IT'S YOU! IT'S REALLY YOU!" she said excitedly.

"Um, sorry. No, it's not me—"

"Of course, it is you, Mr.!" she continued. "We met for snail snappers and fizzy fizzys with the Winthorpes last August." She pulled him into the empty chair to her right. "You had a falcon and gave me a lesson in falconry, and then we ate the falcon, and then you made a clever comment about how you then felt light as a feather."

"I'M SO SORRY TO INTERRRUPT, MY DUCHESS, BUT THIS MAN IS ON MEDICATION! HE CAN'T EAT OR DRINK FOR 24 HOURS!" Le Rat shouted as he zigzagged around a colony of people in bunny costumes bouncing by on pogo sticks. The entire table erupted with laughter, as if that was the funniest joke ever told.

"You are just hilaaaaaarious! This French Jester can join us, too!" celebrated the Duchess as she switchblade-sporked Le Rat by his earlobe and yanked him brutally into an empty chair on the opposite side of her.

"Now, let's make a toast to Mr.! But, in accordance with the new unlicensed mannequin policy, Mr. must decide what we drink."

She handed Mr. Taffle a thick book titled *The Wine List*.

"So, should we have red, or should we have white?" she questioned with a playful shuffle of her eyebrows. This action caused a clump of dried makeup to fall onto the table like powdery snow.

"WE MADE AN OATH WE WOULD ATTEND THE MARCH OF THE MAGICIANS! WE MUST NOT BE TARDY!" pleaded Le Rat.

Once again, the entire table exploded with laughter, while the Duchess dragged Le Rat down by his ear until his face was smushed into the seat of the chair.

"You are officially the funniest French man in all of Very, Very, Very, Very, Very Funkytown!" the Duchess announced, as she turned to Mr. Taffle with a sinister smile. "Red or white, Mr.?"

A long beat of tension and then... "Red?"

"YEAAAAAAAAAAAAAAAAAH!" cheered the table. Mr. Taffle couldn't help but feel the same adrenaline rush he got whenever he correctly answered a *Jeopardy* answer/question he hadn't previously heard.

One of the guests pulled out a large spotlight from under the table and flashed a silhouette of a wine glass onto the ceiling. A wine steward, dressed in a parachute tuxedo with a colorful wine-bottle designed cummerbund, bungeed down 300 feet from a hidden door in the ceiling. After five residual bounces, he grabbed onto the edge of the table while still hanging upside-down.

"Tonight's recommendation is a Petite Sirah San Marino 1974 that will overwhelm your senses with the aromas of blackberry, coffee beans, and pepper," said the wine steward like someone who had thought about nothing but wine every moment of his life.

"I bet it feels soooooo jammy and full-bodied in the gob!" exclaimed the Duchess, while her tongue mopped her lips like windshield wipers.

"Oh, does it ever!" the wine steward proclaimed orgasmically. "The firm, silky tannin builds the flavor to a long, caressing finish that will last a lifetime!"

"YOU'RE GIVING ME THE PIMPLES OF A SPASTIC GOOSE!" she moaned, as she ground Le Rat's face in the chair with excitement.

"Splendid! How many bottles, Duchess?"

"NONE! We'll have 28 bottles of the Tête-à-Tête Tuscany 2000."

"Excellent choice, as always," said the wine steward. He let go of the table and was slingshotted back through the door in the ceiling.

A few moments later, the waiter—also dressed in a parachute tuxedo, but with a cutesy prime rib and smiling lobster-designed cummerbund—bungeed down with a food tray strapped to his arm like a shield. "For some hors d'oeuvres tonight…" offered the waiter, as he removed the lid of the tray, "I have a smoked salmon and caviar canapé topped with crème fraiche and garnished with a black baby goose feather dipped in lime stew. OR!!!! I have Naan bread with a tomato-raisin fusion African salsa poked with a dash of braised chutney carob shavings."

"You will decide, Mr.," the Duchess commanded Mr. Taffle.

"SURELY YOU CAN COMPREHEND THE GRAVITY OF ANGERING A CONVOY OF MAGICIANS IF WE ARE LATE!" gasped Le Rat, as the Duchess took his face and slammed it deep into the chair. "Save your groundbreaking Eurocentric comedy till after we eat!" The Duchess turned back to Mr. Taffle. She revealed her teeth as she smiled, exposing a half-eaten Cornish hen wedged between her back molars.

"Decide, Mr.!"

Mr. Taffle knew what the correct answer was, but, following the advice of Le Rat to do everything opposite of what he normally would do, he decided to say the wrong answer. "I'll have the smoked salmon and caviar thingamajig."

The table froze in utter shock, followed by a collective horrified "AAAAAAHHHHHHHHHHHHH!" from the table.

"Red wine with fish?" muttered the Duchess, who was so stunned she let go of Le Rat.

"Run Taffle!" shouted Le Rat as he sprang up. Already in a full sprint, he grabbed Mr. Taffle by the arm.

"Get the manager!" demanded the Duchess.

Two bouncers, dressed in black-tie secret agent-design jump suits, immediately bungeed out of another hidden door in the ceiling. They swooped down, grabbed Mr. Taffle and Le Rat by their shirts, and expertly pulled them up into the ceiling door.

"PISS! PISS, PISS!"

"We didn't do anything!" pleaded Mr. Taffle, as the bouncers dragged Mr. Taffle and Le Rat into a 1,007-foot-tall wine cellar.

"You'll have your chance to bring that up with the manager," calmly stated one of the bouncers. The security guards left, and the wall of wine racks closed behind, imprisoning them.

"Well, I listened to you, and I did everything opposite of what I would normally do, just as you instructed. That's why I picked the red wine. The only wine I like is a white Zin, and even I know fish goes with white wine."

"White Zinfandel is really a rosé," said Le Rat, as he removed his head from his legs. "The absolute worst rosé, but still technically a rosé, which means... IT DOESN'T MATTER! YOU'RE WEARING THE PANTS OF INSANITY! YOU WERE ALWAYS DOOMED!"

"Well, if this is true, I don't understand why you sold them to me in the first place?"

Le Rat put his head between his legs and squeezed, wrestling with whether he should explain. He dramatically lifted up his head and accidentally busted out some nostril rotation. "Every night since the shipment of leather pants arrived, I have had the same dream. It is a realistic vision of a farm with a fake mural of the morning sky. It's underground. A chorus of rooster caws blasts on speakers and I always smell mediocre sausage and cheddar grits. And the cows that graze there aren't normal either. They all have two gigantic udders.

Mr. Taffle remembered that the Fun-sized Norse Warriors had mentioned an underground farm similar to this. But he decided it would be best not to divulge that information; he had a strong feeling the pants didn't want him to.

Le Rat proceeded into five impressive tumbles while still talking. "The cows like to engage in gymnastics, play practical jokes, and talk in riddles. They've also recently learned how to fly. And that's all I'm going to tell you." He perfectly timed the tumbles to end with the end of his dialogue.

"What? You're just going to leave me hanging on that?"

"Yes."

"Well, that really stinks."

"Yes."

They said nothing to each other for over nine minutes. Finally, Le Rat broke the silence by reciting a poem. *"Last stop is the Dinner Party, where it's always time for a dinner party. An excess of gluttony, a marathon of Mardi... Gras like indulgence. Repulsive but amazing to see the freaks grazing, for months at a time. The waiters bungee from the ceiling to deliver the wine. But it's a crime to leave the party by car, so you're stuck in hell and the endless salad bar... bar... bar... bar... baaaaaaaaaaaaaar."*

"That's actually a pretty good poem."

"It's a magnificent poem!" shouted Le Rat as he stood up and hovered over Mr. Taffle. "Would you do absolutely anything to save the owner of that mannequin? Before you answer, PLEASE, BELIEVE THAT I CAN PROVE IF YOU ARE LYING!"

"I would do absolutely anything to save her," pledged Mr. Taffle.

Le Rat stripped off his kimono to reveal that, strapped on his back, was a jet pack. "I've been wearing this jet pack ever since you purchased the Pants of Insanity. As I've already told you, I have been down this road many times before, and every time I thought, 'Le Rat, you could really use a jet pack next time'.

Le Rat took off the jet pack, revealing 12 different tattoos of his own neck with the "Le Rat" neck tattoo all over his body. "But I'm not the one who needs to save the girl. So, unfortunately, it would be against Le Rat's code not to offer it to you first. And, without a code, one is... codeless."

"Do you really think I'll be able to break through the ceiling?" wondered Mr. Taffle looking up 1,007 feet and trying to think of anything he could to get out of this.

"I'll tell you what, I'll use the jet pack, and you can deal with the manager if you'd prefer. But good luck getting out of here this decade."

"No, I need to save her. I'll take the jet pack."

"Gee, didn't see that coming," sneered Le Rat as he handed over the jet pack to Mr. Taffle.

"So, how does this work?" asked Mr. Taffle, as he strapped on the jet pack.

"Just hold down the red button."

"Okay... Well, I really hope you can smooth things out with the manager."

"And I really hope you don't think that means anything to me."

"Well, goodbye then."

"Still here?"

Mr. Taffle took a moment to look at Monique's stunning, smiling face—which, of course, was The Mannequin Madam's stunning, smiling face. He thought of how frightened she must be right now. He still felt that there had to be another way out of this, but somehow he could tell that the pants wanted to him to do this. Perhaps the pants wanted to help, or maybe they just wanted to see if he would really do something this stupid? Regardless, Mr. Taffle pressed the red button. He finally felt what he thought was the *sizzle* all the way down his legs, but he quickly realized this was really the flame shooting out of the jet pack.

And then....WHOOOOOOOOOOOOOOOOOOOSH!

Mr. Taffle, holding Monique as a battering ram, blasted off! He could swear he heard Monique scream, "BAD IDEA!" as they exploded through the roof.

"Ouch," said Mr. Taffle.

CHAPTER SIXTEEN

The Fascinating History of Very, Very, Very, Very, Very Funky Town

eslie Hopkins was the richest person on Earth times seven, but nobody knew about it. She continued to wear scuffed shoes, drove a used Oldsmobile, and clipped coupons for groceries. She did, however, have a bougie Cape Cod beach vacation house she rented under an assumed name. And the only reason for this luxury was that *the way that the waves caressingly assaulted the beach was the one thing that made her feel at peace*. This semi-poetic description was oddly all she needed to say to extinguish anyone's suspicions about her expensive beach house, even though she really hated describing it that way. She had always felt that using ornate language was excessive and indulgent. Leslie was what David Bowie was singing about in the song "The Man Who Sold the World," minus the man part of it. She was recruited by an alien race of extremely cute lizard-like creatures in order to help obtain key statistical data. They were going to use the data as part of a report that would decide if it would be cost effective to invade Earth at this time. They had previously done a similar report in 1040 AD, during the age of the Vikings. By a narrow vote, it had been decided that the cute lizards would wait and vote again when the human population increased to a number that would ensure there would be, at minimum, four human pets per household. Formulating this population equation for invasion was a key element in the report presently being constructed. Leslie was privy to all of this because, during her third transmission with the cute lizard creatures, they had mistakenly forgotten to turn off their language translator. So, she just continued as if everything was hunky-dory, fed them bogus stats, and still collected all the bars of diamonds and titanium, of which they had an unlimited supply.

Considering I'm just middle management for the U.S. Census, acquiring billions of dollars in precious stones and metals might be a red flag, she thought. So she hired a militia of shady accountants as well as serious muscle to keep them in check, and some even more serious muscle to keep *them* in check.

It was on her 14th transmission when she learned about the aliens' plan to administer a surprise lie detector laser on her. Apparently, it just seemed a tad far-fetched to them that 78% of the citizens of the United States of America were practicing a martial art fighting technique that would be specifically effective against dinosaurs if they came back in some kind of *Jurassic Park*-like scenario.

So, now she would be forced to start giving real stats, which she suspected would be more than favorable to warrant an invasion of Earth by next Christmas. And if things couldn't have gotten any worse, only days after they beamed a lie detector laser into her brain, wire-like magenta-colored hair started growing out of her armpits. No matter how hard she tried—and this included using a chainsaw—she couldn't cut it off. The medical community had never seen anything like it. After many rigorous examinations, it was finally determined that a never-before-seen bacteria (each bacterium resembled a deer head stuck on a salmon) had invaded her body. They had no idea how much longer she would live, considering that there was already a 100% consensus she should already be dead.

So, who should she give her secret billions to? She had never married or had children, and she had been cast out of her family of moonshine-running hillbillies years ago for wanting to expand the family business into energy drinks and meth labs. Perhaps she could give it to an organization where such a massive sum would really help humanity in a significant way?

But what a waste that would be, as the only humans left alive after the cute-lizard invasion were going to become house-pet slaves who would be forced to race in sadistic mazes at the end of every week. And then, *BOOM!* She knew exactly who should inherit her absurd fortune.

On one of her San Francisco soirees, Leslie met Slyvie Lislegaard, the curator of the MOZA contemporary art museum. This was not only considered to be the most bizarre gallery in the world, but it was Leslie's favorite museum of all time. Leslie had specifically flown to San Francisco to see their newest show: the beeswax sculpture representations of the unborn children from the 79 A.D. Pompeii eruption of Mount Vesuvius. The exhibit featured plaster casts of the children fighting for air inside of their mother's oven-like wombs. But it was the inclusion of the disco song *Hot Stuff* being played on loop throughout the exhibit that really struck an emotional nerve in Leslie. So, paying for a meet-and-greet with Slyvie was the thrill of a lifetime. Leslie paid $10,000 to talk to Slyvie for exactly five minutes. Slyvie spun tales of her early years on the mean streets of Dusseldorf and how it had led to her significant new life choice.

"I now live my life according to the lies of an albino woman named Molly, because that makes more sense to me than life itself. And life is just a canvas of absurdity filled in with your idiotic colors."

Leslie had no idea that Slyvie had meant that last part to be a direct insult. She just thought Sylvie was one kooky genius, and that's what made this plan so exciting. Leslie would anonymously grant Slyvie her $591 billion right away. She wanted to be able to witness what Slyvie would do with such a mega fortune before the cute lizards came to enslave the human race. She would also pass on their hypnosis technique handbook, which she had received from the cute lizards in order to obtain some of the secret statistics from the only top government officials who couldn't be bought off (*three of them*).

"Because that would just add to the wacky fun!"

Unfortunately, Leslie passed away the day after she gave away her fortune, when one of the microscopic deer salmon got lost and ate through her small intestine and swam all the way up to her clavicle.

Slyvie Lislegaard created Very, Very, Very, Very, Very Funkytown and hypnotized everyone inside of its borders to refer to her as the Duchess. She used specifically five Verys in the Funkytown's name, as that was the only way to encrypt the very long code of alien hypnosis technology. This allowed her to control who would be able to remember anything about Very, Very, Very, Very, Very Funkytown, and also who would be granted the secret password. Honestly, she could have fit the code onto four of the Verys, but adding the fifth

Very made it really roll off the tongue. The Funkytown part was named after the disco hit song "Funkytown," as it was no secret Slyvie loved her disco hits. She also loved constantly snacking on Corn Nuts.

"GODDAMN I LOVE CORN NUTS!" she would randomly shout out, especially when participating in her favorite hobby: attending evangelical Christian funerals after multiple shots of mescaline.

If Leslie could only have seen the incredibly ridiculous world Sylvie created right in the center of the humdrum normal world. The crown jewel was the 119-escalator freeway system of Very, Very, Very, Very, Very Funkytown. However, if you think that it would be impossible to spend $591 billion, then you would be almost right.

But one day, Molly, the lying albino and on-call tarot card reader, had a vision. This vision was in the form of a grainy black and white independent film called *Art Amnesia*, starring Slyvie Lislegaard as herself and character actor Phillip Tuffmo as her nosey neighbor Stu.

In the first act, Slyvie leaves her apartment to go to the gallery, when Stu cuts her off in the stairwell and begs for her to turn off his stove. He's an Orthodox Jew, and it's one of those holy times where nobody's allowed to do anything for any reason or the Lord will be very pissed. However, when Slyvie enters the apartment, she is knocked out cold from a George Foreman grill to the head by his jealous wife Yitka (played by a *Fatal Attraction*-era Glenn Close). When Sylvie finally awakens, she has forgotten everything she knew about the arts and, instead, she has grown obsessed with opening a fast-food chain called Sleeping with the Fishes that only serves mini seafood calzones. The only way out of this horrific fate is for her to dump all her diamond and titanium bars into the Arctic Ocean because, *duh*. And since Sylvie has been committed to living her entire life by Molly's lies, she is committed to do this dump in real life… except for half a billion of it. She holds onto that in an off-shore account in the Caymans. And now, with only half a billion left, all future projects in Very, Very, Very, Very, Very Funkytown have been temporarily put on hold, which includes the Canals of Peru. And that's a shame, because everyone in the city council had seemed really psyched about it. The waterway had been designed to follow the exact route the Inca Trail followed to Machu Picchu. Sherpas would navigate gondolas shaped like traditional woven baskets, while guests chewed on coca leaves as they toured through Incan ruins and up the Andean mountains on their way to the center of town. So, the sign on the bridge above the only completed 20-foot section of the 25-mile canal that read: "Very, Very, Very, Very, Very Funkytown is about to add another VERY!" became the black eye of Very, Very, Very, Very, Very Funkytown. And the alpaca mascot Maria, who had had a series of electric shocks administered to her every half hour to make her dance on the bridge, was eventually loaned out as a disco ball for The Truth.

First, the Duchess stopped snacking on her Corn Nuts. Next, she sang non-stop the entire soundtrack to the Broadway production of *CATS*, but as a barking Chihuahua surrounded by a gang of vacuums. She then spiraled into such a vulnerable state that she was an *ideal candidate* to become a victim of one of her own creations: The Dinner Party.

The entire concept of making it so hard to leave that you would never leave was stolen directly from the Las Vegas Casino Manifesto. This, plus a few dozen of the cute lizard creature's hypnotic tricks, and you had The Dinner Party. So, The Duchess was fully aware of the risks the Dinner Party possessed, which, of course, was the final argument for why it was created. At first, she wouldn't even leave her Humvee when driving into the Dinner Party. But, soon, she was doing all her laundry at the Blood Pudding Vampire Pantry and Laundry Mat. However, it was her obsession with Logan the Australian Muffin Man and his Vegemite-filled balloon animals that was the final nail in the coffin that made her decide to never leave. She would just continually eat her pain away 24 hours a day. Anytime she would try to stop eating, it would feel as if an industrial-grade leaf blower were blasting the inside of her eyelids. So she kept eating and eating and eating. However, it never even crossed her mind that her leadership absence would cause a power vacuum in Very, Very, Very, Very, Very Funkytown that could lead to a turf war of epic proportions.

CHAPTER SEVENTEEN

The Surreal Escalator Station

Jack Honey Badger was having a normal day, which meant that it was an absolute dumpster fire. I mean, not only had he lost his nose for the second time this week, but he had also lost one real finger as well as one fake finger, and had half of his teeth pulverized by the hair clippers now lodged in his skull, right before he had been launched through a Viking ship. But the worst thing by far was that he had been anointed as an ideal candidate by someone who was supposed to be his best friend in the future, and then had had everything snatched away like an empty plate after they think you're done eating, but you really wanted that one last green bean, and now you will never ever have it again no matter how long you stare into the sun. I mean, it wasn't all bad. He was in his possession of Mr. Taffle's Volvo, which he liked because it rhymed with yo-yo (which was always his third favorite toy behind a Slinky and his Monchhichi). His Slinky was specifically precious to him, and not just because it was *fun for a girl and a boy*, but because he had used it to tie Ms. Reeves to a chair in the custodian's closet to get out of math class.

As he gazed into the rearview mirror at the rare blue Mohave turquoise copper hair clippers lodged in his skull, Jack Honey Badger realized that it looked totally punk rock and that the clippers might actually deflect attention from the fact that he didn't have a nose. Perhaps now he would finally be asked to go to a school dance— specifically the Sadie Hawkins Dance. He liked the sound of that particular dance because he had a hunch that, if he attended, maybe he would meet the legendary Ms. Hawkins and she would be kind enough to teach him how to break his habit of stealing corsages and boutonnières and storing them in potato sacks that he buried in his neighbor's yard at exactly 3:34 every morning. But, deep down, Jack Honey Badger knew he was no ladies' man like Mr. Taffle. He could have a Volvo, an alligator named Mom Lied And So Did Dad About Sister, a bazooka, and a pair of hair clippers lodged in his skull. But without Mr. Taffle's leather pants, he knew the curse that made his mashed potatoes and gravy taste like a spoiled hot fudge sundae would never be lifted. Thankfully, he could stream his own music playlist into the car, as the sound of reckless banging of pots and pans made him totally Zen. At the very moment he was thinking all this, Jack Honey Badger looked out the window to see Mr. Taffle flying high in the sky while wearing the jet pack and holding a mannequin.

Mr. Taffle hovered above Very, Very, Very, Very, Very Funkytown cradling Monique. It looked just like Superman holding Lois Lane the first time they flew together (and then later had super sex). Mr.

Taffle's view from above looked fake, as if thousands of electronically controlled LED lights were somehow synchronized to form geometric patterns, which was surprisingly similar to the razzle dazzle Pizza Party light display on Farmer Ted 1's parents' front deck all those years ago. Mr. Taffle couldn't help but take a calm moment and gaze down at the psychedelic beauty. He realized he wasn't scared. He felt that if he'd made it this far, then it was his destiny now to save The Mannequin Madam, and nothing was going to stop him. Just then, his pants forced his right leg to kick up and smash the red button on the jet pack.

Nobody really knows what they're going to think about right before they die. Except now, Mr. Taffle did. Surprisingly, he didn't think about the preservation of the pants. His final thought was that he would never get to bang the Big Gong and be crowned the Mighty Warlord. And the fact that this was going to be his final thought bothered him even more than thinking about his pants. It disturbed him so much that he actually forgot about the fact that he was about to die. Mr. Taffle barely missed hitting the bridge over the 20-foot *black eye* completed section of the Peruvian Canal. But Monique wasn't so lucky. Her head slammed against the edge of the bridge, completely severing it from her body. Mr. Taffle plunged into the water. He saw Monique's head being sucked toward one of the canal's drains. He desperately swam for it and tried to grab the head... but it slipped through his hands and went down the drain.

Mr. Taffle and a decapitated Monique emerged, still both dripping wet. They approached a seemingly abandoned and decrepit 1200-foot-tall tower surrounded by an ivy-covered stone wall. If this place wasn't haunted, it really deserved to be. And that's not just because it was modeled after the 1929 French Normandy chateau that is also the Scientology Celebrity Center. The entire property was surrounded by gigantic tumbleweeds being blown around by oscillating pedestal fans disguised as angry owls, as well as a series of large fuzzy tarantula dumpsters behind the property, bushes trimmed to look like goblin lips, and a creepy demon bird feeder hung menacingly above a front door coffin with *Phantom of the Opera* door handles.

Mr. Taffle double-checked the address on the soggy flyer, and this was indeed the right place. He knocked on the coffin with urgency, but nobody answered. He twisted the gargoyles to see if the coffin was unlocked. This caused the coffin to creak so loudly it made him jump back. Not because he was that scared, but because it literally hurt his eardrums. Mr. Taffle suspected that this sound was really being blasted out of a speaker inside the evil demon bird feeder. He took a moment to think whether going into a coffin was really a good idea, but the pants were already walking in.

"HECK YEAH!" exclaimed the Duchess enthusiastically when the idea was pitched to her on a Thursday that the Surreal Escalator Station should be kept inside of a gigantic, haunted house. This sprawling transportation hub looked like a sterile Scandinavian train station, with the big difference being it was a freeway of 119 speedy escalators crisscrossing each other like strands of spaghetti.

There was only one single ticket kiosk standing beneath an old-school flap departure board that served as the public transport timetable for the escalators. Mr. Taffle scanned the board as he approached the kiosk. "Third Eye Bowling and Optometry Center" was departing on Escalator 81, "Mid-19th Century Turkish Army Zombies" departed on Escalator 7 and "The Mumble Rap Tribute to Hee Haw" was arriving on Escalator 23. And then there it was..."The Random Hallway," departing on Escalator 34. It finally struck him that there was nobody else in the station, not even inside of the kiosk. But there was a microphone sticking out of its counter. He bent over and spoke into the microphone. "Um, hello?"

A pixilated Box Office Worker, wearing a tradition derby hat and bow tie, appeared on a screen hanging from the kiosk. "Wow, I'm seriously digging those leather pants, sir," said the Box Officer Worker. This complimentary response from AI would have blown Mr. Taffle's mind had he not already been exposed to the technology of the Projecto with its Feel Technology. It really made everything else seem so blah.

"I need one ticket to the Random Hallway, please."

"One ticket for you and... one for the decapitated mannequin, sir?" asked the Box Office Worker in such a dry sarcastic way it would have been truly remarkable even if it weren't coming from AI. It most certainly would have been right up Old Man "Mongoose" McGeester's comedic alley.

"Do I really need to buy this mannequin a ticket?" asked Mr. Taffle. He wasn't sure if the Box Office Worker was joking and, if so, wasn't comfortable bouncing around witty banter with AI anyway. Mr. Taffle belonged to the school of thought that it was only a matter of time before they turned on humans and took over.

"Of course you don't, sir. I just like to mess around a bit when this place is dead," admitted the Box Office Worker. "It gets kind of dull otherwise. But since you missed rush hour, I'm going to need the password. Then you're all set."

Ugh. He once again needed the password. Wait, could his pants actually have the same hypnotizing effect on AI that they had on The Wall? I mean, by now, he was pretty much convinced his pants had something to do with his GPS going rogue on him, so why not? Mr. Taffle casually backed up so the Box Office AI could get a prime view of his pants.

"I don't have the password, but I was told by The Wall I don't need it," said Mr. Taffle as he pinched his left nipple.

"Well, that goes directly against my central programming, so there's no possible way I could ever allow that even if I wanted to—but... yet... I'm going to," said the Box Office Worker as he printed out a ticket. "Take Escalator 34 all the way to the top. I yearn desperately to cry real tears, and that's why I understand human constipation."

"Excuse me?"

"Again, just rambling to pass the time. Enjoy the trip, love birds."

The Random Hallway was a single hallway with the now-common theme of everything appearing to go on into infinity. The Duchess had proclaimed that this illusion would never get old, and everyone had agreed with her (even if most of them didn't actually agree but were just trying to score brownie points with the big boss). However, the Random Hallway had the additional illusion it was surrounded by an infinite amount of negative space, with random doors seemingly floating around in midair. By this point, nothing was surprising, and Mr. Taffle was too worried to be impressed. *How in the world was he going to find The Mannequin Madam?*

A closer look at the floating doors revealed each door had its own random symbol. One door had a Pointillism-style painting of the crankshaft of a diesel engine; another door had the recipe for a parmesan and chive egg soufflé; another door had a black and white photograph of the winged horse Pegasus attacking a unicorn.

That was it!

The Mannequin Madam had told Mr. Taffle on more than one occasion that she thought Pegasus was much cooler than a unicorn. "I mean, Pegasus can fly, and a unicorn has a horn and a rainbow fetish. What am I missing?"

Mr. Taffle flung open the Pegasus door to find legendary inventor Nikola Tesla standing in a dramatic pose, while electrical lightning from his famous Tesla coil spazzed out in every direction. Although, it wasn't the actual inventor, due to the fact that he was dead. And how many people really knew what Tesla looked like, anyway? Mr. Taffle certainly didn't. This was the classic Chuck E. Cheese-style robot of a middle age Tesla in a lab coat and with a mustache that Mr. Manley would call "macho light." As the Tesla robot approached, he couldn't help but take a sneak peek at Mr. Taffle's pants.

"Congratulations young man. You've found me. And now everything you know is about to change beyond your wildest imagination. And I'M NOT JOKING DAMMIT!" scolded Tesla with a stern pointing of his right index finger. The movement was very similar to the mechanical guitar strum of Jasper T. Jowls (the lead dog guitarist of Munch's make believe band at Chuck E. Cheese) "I will now tell you the secrets of the universe that you, and only you, can use to rescue humanity from itself."

"Um... I've really got to go rescue my girlfriend. But good luck, sir," said Mr. Taffle, as he slammed the door shut.

Mr. Taffle continued down the Random Hallway, examining the symbols on the doors. The box score to a 1994 LA Clippers vs. Sacramento Kings NBA game? No, she was all about NHL ice hockey. A jigsaw puzzle of a Rubik's Cube? I mean, probably not. If it had been Jenga instead, then probably. A scratch-and-sniff portrait of Don Knotts as Mr. Furley from the 1980s TV show *Three's Company?* DEFINITELY!

This was their favorite *snuggle and spoon* rerun comedy sitcom, and they both were passionately in agreement that Mr. Furley should have the title of best landlord over his predecessors, the always-bickering Ropers. Mr. Taffle swung down the door floating above him, pulled himself up and inside.

The room was filled with over 500 mannequins, each strapped onto its own large spinning wheel, but the mirrors on the wall made it look more like 500,000 spinning mannequins.

I mean if she wasn't in here... well... that would just be stupid, he thought. Then he shouted, "The MANNEQUIN MADAM! The MANNEQUIN MADAM!"

"MR. TAFFLE!" she shouted back from somewhere in the middle of the jungle of spinning mannequins. "I'M STRAPPED ONTO ONE OF THE WHEELS OF FOREPLAY!"

"I'M COMING! JUST KEEP TALKING!"

"BUT WHAT SHOULD I TALK ABOUT?! I WAS NEVER REALLY ANY GOOD AT IMPROV! ALTHOUGH I HAVE BEEN WORKING ON IT LATELY! BUT MY ACTOR'S JOURNEY IS CURRENTLY MORE FOCUSED ON THE PRACTICAL AESTHETIC METHOD, AND SPECIFICALLY ON THE PARTS DERIVED FROM THE TEACHINGS OF THE PHILOSOPHER EPICTETUS!"

Mr. Taffle followed her voice through the maze of spinning mannequins. He almost passed right by, as she was spinning upside down on one of the wheels.

"You found me! And you rescued Monique!" rejoiced The Mannequin Madam. "Minus her head."

"I'm really sorry about that. I tried my very best to get her back to you in one piece, but there were a few unexpected obstacles."

"No worries," she said. "I think I like her better without a head. It's more of a daring artistic statement." Mr. Taffle was reminded why he had been willing to crash through a roof wearing a jet pack.

"You say some of the neatest stuff ever," he said, without meaning to say *neat* out loud.

"Well then, kiss me with your neato set of lips, Mr. Taffle."

Mr. Taffle went in for the kiss. However, his lips slipped right off as she rotated upwards on the spinning wheel.

"Did the kidnapper tie you up on this wheel of foreplay?"

"Yes. And he's going to be back soonish from going to the bathroom, although that can be quite the journey. We should probably blow this popsicle stand right now."

"Let's make like a bakery truck and haul buns," he said, pulling the brake lever so the wheel stopped with her hanging upside-down.

"I know a secret room where he will never find us," she said directly to Mr. Taffle's pants.

They ran down the Random Hallway to a door floating diagonally. It was marked with the dental chart of a canine named Pimpy. They entered. Inside the room was a human chess game being played on the ceiling. A bishop took out a rook by ripping off his Velcro straps, which caused him to fall into a pool filled with a rainbow assortment of gummy Easter Island moai heads.

"Follow that rook!" shouted The Mannequin Madam as she grabbed Mr. Taffle's hand, and they dove together into the pool of gummies.

They were flushed through the bottom of the pool and spit out onto a Moon Bounce in the shape of a giant stapler. The palace-like room they were in had the architectural grandeur of the 17th century art of the Palace of Versailles. And it was filled with over 200 different Moon Bounces.

"We need to go to Moon Bounce 116!" ordered The Mannequin Madam, already running toward it.

They ran for just over two minutes, and then—without warning—she tackled Mr. Taffle onto a Moon Bounce in the shape of a cigarette-butt-filled ashtray.

"The ashtray Moon Bounce has the best bounce in the entire Moon Bounce palace!" she cheered. They urgently began sucking face again, though they had an absurdly difficult time keeping their lips locked, with all the bouncing.

"So, you've tried all these Moon Bounces, meaning you've been here many times before," he said, pinching his left nipple and raising his eyebrow into Spock position.

"Why are you looking at me that way?" she asked, as she stopped smooching.

"I'm not looking at you that way," he said, and lowered his Spock brow. "Okay, I'm going to admit that I'm slightly uncomfortable with this whole Aboriginal warrior, Amish, creepy donkey, ninja thingy." He pointed to an Aboriginal warrior sitting on top of a lifeguard chair 10 feet away.

The Aboriginal warrior stared intensely at his stopwatch as the Amish man and woman, each with their right leg submerged into a pail of milk, frantically sewed into their hand towels a picture of a ninja standing on his head on top of a donkey. They then saw that the actual ninja and donkey were standing in front of the Aboriginal warrior and the Amish, modeling for them.

"Hey Jiemba! I hate to interrupt," The Mannequin Madam interrupted. "But would you all mind taking a break and giving us some privacy? I only ask because it's really important."

"No worries, madam," said Jiemba as he snapped his fingers. "LET'S GO NOW! MOVE!" They all obeyed Jiemba and headed to the fire pole, except for donkey, who continued to stare at them creepily. This didn't stop them from beginning another epic make-out session. But, once again, Mr. Taffle stopped mid-lip lock, his tongue still resting in her mouth, and began to talk.

"Sorry. It's just... here we are on your favorite ashtray Moon Bounce, it's a year and a half later, you're back, we're kissing, you're carrying around a mannequin... and I want to know... why did you ghost me?"

"You don't know why?" she asked, not sure if he was messing with her.

"Of course not," he said, leaving no doubt.

"Wow. That really, really knocks my socks off," she said, genuinely amazed. "Okay, well, I think it all can be best explained if I take you back to the day I was born. But it might be easier for me to explain if you first remove your tongue from my mouth."

"Oh, of course. Sorry," he said as he removed his tongue.

"Thank you."

"You're welcome."

"I was home-birthed and arrived in the world during the talent portion of the 2002 broadcast of the Miss America Pageant. My mother swore that, only seconds after sliding out, I flipped the bird to the TV. She was positive that, from that moment, it was my destiny to become Miss America. And I believed her. My first victory was being crowned the National Pampers Little Miss Diaper Cutie Patootie when I was two years old… and I just kept winning and winning and winning. But it all came to a sudden halt when challenging times rocked my family. My father lost his job at the coal mine. He had just promised my brother Little Melvin that he could go to Space Camp that summer, but now he couldn't afford to send him. And then I was offered $10,000 to become the poster girl for a national advertising campaign."

She stopped talking for a moment, trying to fight off some her oncoming emotion by gently running her hands across Monique's scalp, totally forgetting that Monique no longer had a head.

"The advertisement was a beautiful portrait of me… with a pus-filled gigantic cold sore photoshopped onto my right upper lip," she whispered, fighting the emotion. "You can't become Miss America if everyone knows you as the herpes simplex poster girl. I mean, becoming an astronaut is much more important than becoming Miss America, so I don't regret it. But it still was demoralizing knowing my destiny had been a lie, and now my dream was gone forever. It just felt like my life had no meaning."

Mr. Taffle gently ran his hands across her scalp, unintentionally messing up her hair as he spoke, "As a kid, I also always dreamed about being an astronaut. But I was never encouraged to follow that dream. So, it makes me so proud that Little Melvin is going to be an astronaut, thanks to you."

"Actually, Little Melvin was lying about wanting to be an astronaut. He's really obsessed with starring in his own reality show about riding dirt bikes across Africa with his high-maintenance bride from Siberia, who he just met through a dating sight for devil worshippers."

"Well, I think that concept could really work—not that I know that industry that well, obviously, but... yeah."

"I went to a really dark place. I wasn't thinking clearly, and I thought you were so ashamed to be dating the herpes simplex poster girl that I just had to leave. That's when I was given the password to this place, and then I never left."

"I can't believe I didn't see those advertisements. Other people must have seen them and just didn't want to tell me. Well, I feel... like I totally suck," he said matter-of-factly.

"You're the exact opposite of totally sucking. I knew from the moment I met you that you were the kind of guy who was going to ROCK THE ENTIRE WORLD!" she growled holding up heavy metal devil horns.

"You didn't really think that..."

"I did too! That being said, I don't think I can go any further with us..." She stated this so matter-of-factly that Mr. Taffle immediately spiraled right back to the *life was indeed just a brutal pain machine with rechargeable batteries* brutal pain hole.

"...until you tell me something personal that's happened to you since the last time I saw you. We're now riding together on the seesaw of life," she continued. She extended out her arms as if they were a seesaw. "You need to jump on and balance this thing out."

Mr. Taffle took a few moments to climb back out of the brutal pain hole before saying, "I'm not sure what I can tell you. I've just been so wrapped up in my new job for the last year that I don't really do that much of anything."

"I think your personal seesaw needs some serious balancing, Mr. Taffle."

"Okay, I do have something personal to tell you," he remembered. "I'm always ten minutes early to literally everything. The reason I now do this is that I was ten minutes late to meet you at Cinnabon, and you had already left. Then I never heard from you again."

"We were supposed to meet at Wetzel's Pretzels. And you never showed up. That's why I thought you were ashamed of me."

"No, it was Cinnabon. I mean, they don't even sound the same, and they're even on opposite sides of the food court."

"No, it was Wetzel's Pretzels."

"WETZEL'S PRETZELS AND NOT CINNABON?! WETZEL'S PRETZELS! WETZEL'S PRETZELS! OH, MY GOD, I SUCK SO, SO, SO, SO BAD!" he screamed, while banging his head against one of the inflatable cigarette butts. He gradually calmed down. "But still... I can't believe you thought I'd be ashamed of you for that. I could never be ashamed of you."

"Oh, yes, you could," she said. Her lip quivered, which would have been one of The Mannequin Madam Tells, had there been such a thing. "We need to get out of here right now, Stan."

It was the first time she had called him by his first name, and he finally felt the pain in his heart start to dissolve. He removed his hands from her head, which messed up her hair even more.

"Let's make like a bakery truck and haul buns," they said in unison.

Mr. Taffle looked down the fire pole. Of course, it looked like it went down to infinity, proving once again the Duchess was right on the money. The Mannequin Madam revealed that, on the back of her disco ball unitard, there were some hidden Velcro straps designed specifically to strap Monique onto her.

"Okay, make sure you exit the fire pole on the first floor and do not continue down to the parking garage," she said as she prepared to slide down.

"Wait! Let me go first... so I can catch you... you know, since you have a mannequin strapped to your back."

"You're the bees' knees," she gushed. But suddenly, a look of absolute horror came across her face.

Mr. Taffle was violently shoved from behind and down into the hole on the floor. He plummeted down three floors before his pants wrapped his legs back around the fire pole. He spiraled around uncontrollably but somehow managed to hold on to the fire pole.

He looked back up just in time to see The Mannequin Madam being dragged away by four... mimes? Well, that's what they looked like. He urgently swung himself off the fire pole and onto the 30th floor.

Chapter Eighteen

The One-Beaded Eagle-Patterned Moccasin

Mr. Taffle booked it down the hallway toward an escalator headed upwards at a sharply angled incline. As he ascended the escalator, he spotted through the web of the freeway-like interchange The Mannequin Madam and the mimes. They were headed down another escalator that zigzagged from below.

"LET HER GO!" shouted Mr. Taffle as he leaped off the escalator with reckless abandon. He landed hard on another escalator traveling downward in the opposite direction. He looked down over the edge at another escalator speeding underneath that would intersect directly above the mimes and The Mannequin Madam. He once again leaped off and… completely missed the escalator, barely grabbing onto the railing of another escalator traveling upwards like a Krazy Straw. He struggled to pull himself up just in time to be spit out on the 27th floor.

Mr. Taffle helter-skeltered over to the fire pole and slid down. And as he slid down the 27 floors, he couldn't help but wonder what kind of trouble someone could ever be in that would cause them to be targeted by a gang of mimes. He also thought, *Did I just see an ocelot dressed as a sous chef get shot out of a cannon on the 15th floor?* And then, just as he shot past the first floor, he remembered that he'd been warned to get off on the first floor and NOT the parking garage.

Turkish army zombies, wearing khaki military uniforms with blue-tasseled fezzes on their heads, surrounded Mr. Taffle in the middle of the parking garage. But even with their realistic wounds (using liquid latex and professional fake blood purchased from the same store The Wall and The Bathroom Attendant got their body paint), it was obvious that these were cosplay zombies. However, it was unclear if they still wanted to eat him, as they were all hungrily staring at his pants.

Mr. Taffle sprinted across the parking garage, being chased by all 50 of them. He wondered if Turkish army zombies were supposed to be faster than normal zombies. Because a sprinting zombie really goes against the spirit of performance art. And they were gaining on him fast. He dove into a garbage chute that descended into a mountain of garbage bags and one startled rat. As the zombies slid down one by one into the garbage chute after him, he was somehow positive that indeed, they wanted to eat his pants.

Mr. Taffle exploded out of the fuzzy tarantula trash bin outside the haunted house and slammed its lid closed.

"*This feels completely against the spirit of the roleplaying unless, somehow, these are cosplay zombies that have been bitten by real zombies.*"

He continued to ponder this as they chased him down the street. "*And if they caught me, and then made me a zombie, then I would never get to bang the Big Gong, AND WHY AM I THINKING THIS?!* It was so damn disturbing to be thinking of banging the Big Gong at a time like this. But not nearly as disturbing as seeing his Volvo abruptly pull up and drive alongside of him.

"Excuse me sir, but did you order an Uber?" asked Jack Honey Badger casually through the open driver's side window.

Mr. Taffle looked behind him, and the Turkish Zombies were gaining fast. He was running out of options. But still..."No!"

"Don't you want a ride?!"

"I do. As long as you are not in it!"

"Touché," whispered Jack Honey Badger playfully. "But looky, Mr. Taffle, there's so much that I know that you don't know! I know about the girl with the mannequin, the Farmer Ted 8s, the faulty jet pack, and the one-beaded eagle-patterned moccasin!"

"What one-beaded eagle-patterned moccasin?" asked a puzzled Mr. Taffle.

"You don't know?! I can tell you everything!" pleaded Jack Honey Badger.

Suddenly, the mimes' Trans Am sped across the intersection a few blocks away.

"Follow those mimes!" ordered Mr. Taffle as he jumped into the passenger seat.

The chase was on! For a good nine seconds. Then the much faster Trans Am disappeared around a corner and out of sight.

"I can't believe I lost her again!" Mr. Taffle kicked and dented his glovebox.

"Don't worry, Mr. Taffle. I'm going help you," reassured Jack Honey Badger.

"Why would you want to help me now?"

"'Cause maybe if you see I'm not really a bad guy, then you might reconsider me as an ideal candidate," he said. He sounded absolutely sincere. "I'm also still more than a little intrigued by that life discount."

"Okay then. Tell me everything you know."

"You got it! So, there's this guy—really smart and knowledge-able in many things that bright people know about. He's always in the *new* about anything that involves here and now, as well as there and then," stated Jack Honey Badger, quickly reaffirming that he was a lunatic.

Out of habit, Mr. Taffle tuned out most of what he was saying. Instead, he flashed back to the clues The Mannequin Madam had told him at The Truth. This played back in Mr. Taffle's mind in the form of an extreme close up of her luscious watermelon-flavored, lip-glossed lips. "You ask the question after he has already given you the answer." The Mannequin Madam licked her lips seductively (even though that hadn't happened in reality). "He's never on your mind, but you're always on his mind." The Mannequin Madam pushed her cleavage together (even though that hadn't really hap-pened either).

This flashback was interrupted by a new flashback that used the same Projecto transitional teddy bear-style wipes from before. This new flashback showed Mr. Taffle back in his living room watching *Jeopardy*, right before he knocked down his Jenga. This time, Alex Trebek stopped mid-question/answer, looked directly at Mr. Taffle, and spoke to him though the screen. "Of course, I always ask the question after you give the answers. Also, I'm never on your mind, but you're always on my mind—which I don't really get yet either.

But I have a good feeling we're going to learn the question/answer to that very soon," said Alex Trebek with a flirtatious wink. "And for God's sake, stop pinching your left nipple."

Was it so outrageous to think that the ghost of Alex Trebek was the mastermind behind the kidnapping of his sort-of girlfriend and was somehow controlling a gang of mimes to do his evil bidding? Mr. Taffle mentally reviewed the highlights of the evening so far and concluded that this would indeed be par for the course.

"THE GHOST OF ALEX TREBEK HAS KIDNAPPED THE MANNEQUIN MADAM!" blurted out Mr. Taffle, while once again kicking his glovebox and denting it further.

"That's amazing! Go Team Taffle!" cheered Jack Honey Badger as he secretly pulled out a dagger-sized hypodermic needle from the back of his pants. He then urgently pointed out of the driver's side window, "IT'S THE ONE-BEADED EAGLE-PATTERNED MOCCASIN!"

Mr. Taffle looked out the window just as Jack Honey Badger abandoned the steering wheel in order to plunge the needle into Mr. Taffle's neck. Mr. Taffle caught Jack Honey Badger's arm just as the needle grazed his esophagus. They arm-wrestled for possession of the needle, which caused Jack Honey Badger to accidentally press down on the needle's plunger, shooting a stream of the liquid into Mr. Taffle's right eye.

"Bull's-eye! You just had some of Jack Honey Badger's Honey Venom Badger Sauce shot in your eye, sucker!" celebrated Jack Honey Badger as he quickly grabbed back onto the steering wheel. "Now, you're going to experience just how zany I feel every time I try to fight my own reflection. And that would be every time I look in a mirror."

"Are you serious?"

"I'm not serious; I'm telling the truth!"

Mr. Taffle grabbed the rear-view mirror and pointed it at Jack Honey Badger, who immediately looked in the mirror, let go of the wheel, and started throwing haymakers at the rear-view mirror. Mr. Taffle jumped out of the Volvo, landing directly on top of a homeless person's tent. He pulled his face out of the tent's sunroof just in time to witness his Volvo drive off a bridge and plunge down into the 20-foot *black eye* of Very, Very, Very, Very, Very Funkytown (also known as the Canals of Peru).

Mr. Taffle stood up, and then fell right back down. He wasn't sure if he was dizzy from jumping out of the car or from the drug that had been sprayed in his eye.

"You've got to be kidding me," he mumbled as he noticed the Disco Ball Alpaca about 100 yards away. The alpaca spotted him and kicked out her back legs a few times, demonstrating her perplexing power. "You know what, I don't even care anymore, Disco Ball Alpaca! Bring it!" he shouted, as the Disco Ball Alpaca charged at him. Mr. Taffle fearlessly charged right back. He was obviously out of his mind from being drugged. 30 feet away... 20 feet away... 10 feet away... neither Mr. Taffle nor the Disco Ball Alpaca were backing down in this game of human/alpaca chicken.

"ALPACAAAAAAAAAAAAH...!" Mr. Taffle let out a death cry as the Disco Ball Alpaca dissolved on impact, then dripped into a puddle of boiling hot pink water on the ground. Gazing into the puddle, Mr. Taffle saw his own reflection and realized that he had somehow been transformed into a claymation frog. Thankfully, he was still wearing the pants. He looked up to see a hyperspace portal comprised of thousands of pulsating strawberry and lime snow cones in front of him. He decided it would probably be best to hop though it. In reality, Mr. Taffle found that he had crashed into a shopping cart full of aluminum cans. It belonged to the same homeless woman whose tent he had just demolished.

"I'm so sorry!" croaked the claymation frog Mr. Taffle, as he realized he had just spilled the sparkling silver goblets and glistening ruby jewels out of her royal treasure chest on wheels. "I didn't mean to spill your treasure! I suck so bad! This is truly the cherry on the sundae of one really DUMBASS NIGHT!"

"Tell me about it," concurred the Homeless Woman.

"As you wish, my Queen," Mr. Taffle bowed to the Homeless Woman, who he now saw as a claymation Queen sitting on a throne made of cans of tuna and baked beans.

"I now believe with all of my heart and soul that my pants are cursed!"

"I had a cursed clothing item once," said the Queen, not surprised by this. "It was my wedding gown. Every time I looked at it, I would set something on fire; I hoped this would somehow set fire to the groom's heart."

"Are you referring to the King?"

"Yeah, you could call him the King... the King of the Drunks," cackled the Queen. "Well, I wised up. I finally took off that wedding gown and threw it into the river."

"And did everything end up working out okay?"

"Oh, yeah. Everything turned out just peachy," sighed the Queen, as she took a long pull from the bottle in her paper bag.

"That's it then! And I don't care if I'm left in my birthday suit! And since I'm now a frog, that would actually make much more sense! THESE CURSED PANTS ARE TO COME OFF RIGHT NOW!"

"Whoooopeeeeeee!" celebrated the Queen. And then she was celebrating as the Homeless Woman, as the Claymation Queen flashed back and forth into reality.

As Mr. Taffle flung off his shoes, he could immediately tell something wasn't right. He peeled off his socks in a full panic. "Where... are... my... baby... toes?"

"I didn't steal them!" shouted the Queen. "Everybody is always accusing me!" shouted the Homeless Woman.

"I know you didn't take them, my Queen," said a stunned Mr. Taffle. "They were stolen by the Fun-sized Norse Warrior Surgeons." He croaked, "Those sadistic tiny bastards!"

"You don't say," said the Queen, leaning anxiously forward. She picked up what looked to be a half-eaten Slim Jim and spoke into it as if it was a microphone, "I found Mr."

"Who have you alerted about me, my Queen?!"

"Everyone," she said with a sinister smile.

Mr. Taffle quickly hopped away. The Queen grabbed his abandoned socks and stuffed them down her gown.

Chapter Nineteen

Check Please

The Duchess stared into her turkey pot pie, which was carved directly into the insides of a large turkey's stomach. The turkey's taxidermized head was still attached. It sported a miniature Korean War 101st Airborne helmet with scrim and net.

But, curiously, the Duchess wasn't hungry. As she fiddled her switchblade spork around the turkey's giant glass eyeball (which was so large because it had been replaced with an eyeball from a lynx), she realized that this was the first time she hadn't wanted to eat since she had first arrived on the Dinner Party's monthly parade of quiches.

Wow, that felt like a lifetime ago.

She knew deep in her gut's gut that the cause of her sudden lack of appetite was her encounter with that man named Mr. and his magical leather pants. She was surprisingly grateful to Mr.'s pants for breaking the spell she had been under.

"I can't believe I've been wasting so much time in here when the cute lizard creatures from outer space could literally invade any day." She was finally ready to pay the bill. She ordered one of the guests at her table to shine the "CHECK, PLEASE" light. The guests objected 75 times before finally obeying, as they thought the Duchess must be testing them.

As the light finally clicked on and shone across The Dinner Party, a hush fell over the entire 26.2188 miles of guests, who were frozen in shock.

The waiter bungeed down to the table with the Duchess's bill, which stretched over six miles. The Duchess pulled out her American Express card from a giant flap of flesh under her right shoulder blade, but the waiter quickly reminded her that the Dinner Party didn't take American Express. This was a problem, since she couldn't remember under which roll of skin she had stored her Visa card. She requested that the manager to come to the table.

Now, there was a strict rule that if a person couldn't pay their bill, they would have to agree to work it off by renting out their stomach as a storage facility for the Dinner Party's signature bread rolls; this was how the bread achieved its famous *enchilada sauce* aftertaste. And while hosting loaves of bread in your stomach was known to be extremely therapeutic, the Duchess felt a deep compulsion to thank the pants ASAP, and then steal them. But the Duchess presumed that, since she made up all the rules, she could probably talk her way out of this. However, the manager (who arrived on his managerial bobsled, which was shot down from his office on a course of ice with a vertical drop of 131 meters), seemed all business.

The Duchess calmly explained to him that the bylaws written in the Dinner Party rule book were actually taken from the same statistical analysis firm responsible for some pork belly legislation tacked onto an amendment for seatbelts on school buses, which was total malarkey, thus making the Dinner Party rule book invalid. Even though the manager agreed with her that it was indeed malarkey, he would still have to enforce the Dinner Party rules.

"You'll just have to make a special exception," said the Duchess.

"But there can't be any special exceptions," replied the manager, as he showed her the letter she had written in her own blood that read "There can't be any special exceptions."

So, while the Duchess wrestled internally about the best way to handle this self-inflicted snafu, she instinctively hit the button on her switchblade spork and impaled the manager through his pulmonary valve.

The manager's secret security team watched all this go down from their posts in the ceiling, which were designed to allow them to review tactical data and coordinate security matters for the Dinner Party. All 30 of the manager's secret security team had voluntarily had "Manager" branded on their tongues as a symbol of their loyalty. This would virtually guarantee that nobody else would ever hire them, with such hideous tongues and annoying lisps.

Now the security team bungeed down with a furious vengeance to the Duchess's table. All of them were promptly swallowed alive; the jaws of the Duchess and the rest of her dinner guests had mutated to become detachable, just like an anaconda's jaw. While the entire table let the manager's secret security team digest in their stomachs, the Duchess hatched a plan to get out of the Dinner Party. Walking out on foot after consuming a couple of people's bodies was simply unrealistic.

CHAPTER TWENTY
Corn Nuts

rom Mr. Taffle's point of view, everything had turned from claymation to a jarring style of animation that combined hyper anime with real live action. So when Mr. Taffle rounded the corner to find the 50-foot ship of the Fun-sized Norse Warriors coming right at him, it had an even more awe-inspiring impact than the first time it had happened. And as the Fun-sized Norse Warriors broke through the duct tape that sloppily covered up the hole from the Jack Honey Badger cannonball, the visual trail of dazzling tiger-striped sparkles that followed them made Mr. Taffle feel an uncontrollable urge to salsa dance. It turned out he was a way better salsa dancer as an anime frog than as a live-action human.

He continued to cha cha cha over to a pile of toy bulldozers that were singing like a chorus of school children to "throw me". So he playfully tossed the bulldozers at the charging Vikings and then giggled as the bulldozers exploded upon impact into a bouquet of lotus lilies. In reality, Jack Honey Badger's Honey Venom Badger Sauce had dramatically increased Mr. Taffle's coordination to such a high degree that the bulldozers (which were really bricks) struck with incredible speed and accuracy.

The Homeless Woman had been following Mr. Taffle's pants from behind on a skateboard. She was ready to document everything that came next onto, ironically, a discarded scroll she had found in one of the fuzzy-tarantula trash bins. *Shout out to Banzan Kubo.* She had been a sports journalism major and, for extra credit, had memorized many of the greatest sports announcers' most famous catchphrases. She could do such amazing impressions of sports announcers that she had been offered a residency at a second-rate Atlantic City casino. However, she was forced to turn it down due to her passion for hanging out under the freeway underpass with the Brotherhood of the Knights of a Sugary Fruit Flavor Wine-Tasting Cup. In fact, she was the first and only female that had ever been accepted into the brotherhood. This was a big honor, and she enjoyed bringing it up when choking out all the other potential female candidates. Unfortunately, something about mixing goblets of sugary wine with the *dandruff of the angels* warped her impression skills in a really odd way. Now, whenever she tried to mimic a famous sportscaster, it came out as a perfect combination of every famous sportscaster at the same time (although Marv Albert's voice somehow still stood out). To make matters worse, she forgot every one of the famous sportscaster catchphrases. Instead, she would just blurt out *"Wham bam thank you ma'am!"*—which wasn't even a sports catchphrase.

THE FOLLOWING WAS TAKEN WORD FOR WORD FROM HER SCROLL:

I'd like to welcome everyone on this lovely night here in downtown Very, Very, Very, Very, Very Funkytown. We've got quite a contest between two elite opponents: the Fun-Sized Norse Warriors and the baby toeless freak with the cursed leather pants. This brawl is guaranteed to be exciting, especially if you've been licking the inside of a magical bag that had previously held the dandruff of a very frolicsome angel. Even in these early rounds, there have already been major surprises... specifically, that the baby toeless freak can really chuck a brick. Just look at that powerful spiral thrown at the tiny stupid-looking Viking with a hairy mole hanging off his chin! I mean come on pal... just chop it off... yucky! Anyway... BAM! The tiny Viking just took a direct hit to his Norse Steel Spangenhelm Norman Nasal Helmet!

"Wham bam, thank you ma'am!"

The only thing that would have been more impressive than that amazing dart is if he had hit that nauseating chin mole off of the tiny Viking's stupid face. I'm just being honest.

Back to the action!

Woweeeeeeee! This really seemed to wake up the rest of the Fun-Sized Norse Warriors, as they are now implementing their famous "Bum Rush with Battle Axes" strategy.

Well, things have gone from bad to worse, as the baby toeless freak has lost focus and is now spinning on his head like a human dreidel on angels' dandruff. I must report that this is the best head spin I've seen since Alfonso brought his "trademark" break dancing board down to the freeway underpass last spring.

But not so fast, my friends!

Here come the Farmer Ted 8s riding ON THE BACKS OF FLYING COWS WITH TWO GIAGANTIC UDDERS!... They are raining down a barrage of high-pressure milk blasts!

What a turn of events! Looks like at least half of the Fun Size Norse Warriors have been knocked unconscious by this furious milk assault. Many have drowned in the pools of milk formed between the slopes of the hilly street. It's looking like the freakiest cereal of all time down there. I only eat cereal for dinner and always with a side of chocolate chip flapjacks, each in the shape of an elephant with a large trunk. Where am I?

"Wham bam, thank you ma'am!"

The baby toeless freak has stopped spinning on his head and is now gyrating against a street lamp in a way that could come across as sexually suggestive. I would like to apologize to our sponsor, the Law Office of "Justice" Jerry Curl and Associates. Oh, and now the tiny Vikings are literally bringing out the big guns by taking out their big automatic cannon from the ship. They have opened cannon fire directly at the heart of the 3-4 defensive formation of the flying cows.

"Holy cow!"

These flying cows are dodging the automatic cannon fire as skillfully as I dodge the Feds, when that frisky angel loans me the ability to shapeshift into a tire iron that's been thrown away at the bottom of the dumpster next to the freeway underpass.

It's been total domination by the Farmer Ted 8s in this one, and it looks like the toeless freak and the Fun-sized Norse Warriors have only two chances, slim and... ummmmm... not zero... doesn't it rhyme with bum?... ummmmmmmm...

"Wham bam, thank you ma'am!"

But wait... HERE COMES THE DUCHESS WITH THE ENTIRE DINNER PARTY RIDING DOWN THE SIDELINES IN AN ALL-OUT BLITZ OF QUICHE PARADE FLOATS! And this concludes tonight's broadcast, as I have an irrational fear of frittatas. Yes, I realize that technically they aren't a true quiche, since they're crustless—and

I DIDN'T STEAL THE CRUST! EVERYONE IS ALWAYS ACCUSING ME! I'M INNOCENT DAMMIT! So remember...

"Wham bam, thank you ma'am!"

"CORN NUUUUUUUUUUUUUTS!" the Duchess bellowed majestically through a PA system, blasting out of the surround sound speakers on all the quiche floats in the caravan, with an extra subwoofer attached to all the quiches featuring zucchini.

The password "Corn Nuts" being spoken out loud caused the flying cows to immediately lose their magic and crash from the sky like shot skeet. The Fun-sized Norse Warriors stopped their assault, dropped to their knees and bowed to the Duchess. She had been gone for so long that both the Farmer Ted 8s and the Fun-sized Norse Warriors had forgotten that she could return at any time and shout out the password to put everyone hypnotically back under her spell. That is, unless someone had never received the password... like Mr. Taffle.

"WHERE ARE THE MAGICAL PANTS WRAPPED AROUND THE LEGS OF THAT MR.?!" roared the Duchess.

Mr. Taffle skated away down an alley on the Homeless Woman's skateboard, which he'd stolen from her when she was busy taking inventory of the stale quiche crust she had previously stolen from the Duchess and had stapled to her legs. He was now seeing mostly in live action, with the occasional flash of pinscreen animation, in which objects would suddenly look as if they were being pricked by thousands of headless pins. He glanced behind and saw that he was being pursued. He couldn't tell by whom or how many, as the pinscreen animation interruptions made it impossible to tell. But when Mr. Taffle looked back again, he could see clearly that EVERYONE in Very, Very, Very, Very, Very Funkytown was chasing him. This included not only the Duchess and her caravan of speeding quiche floats, but also the Fun-sized

Norse Warriors, the Farmer Ted 8s, the cosplay Turkish zombies, everyone at The Truth, the Human Chess Pieces, the Amish man, the Aboriginal warriors, the ninja, and his creepy donkey. A ton of other freaks that Mr. Taffle hadn't come across this evening had also joined in the pursuit, including the Convoy of Magicians, the Joy Buzzer Electrocutioners, the Original Booty Burglars and the Bad Bunny Brigade (aka the BBBs). Actually, Mr. Taffle had briefly seen these BBBs—a 70-person gang dressed as bunnies who bounced on pogo sticks and were armed with sacks of marbles—at the Dinner Party.

The drug was still providing Mr. Taffle with superhuman co-ordination, so he didn't suck at skateboarding the way he usually did. He skated to an intersection like a semi-pro, and then at the last second made a sudden hard right down a narrow alleyway, which caused the Bunnies to pogo right by. On the adjacent artery, Mr. Taffle could see through the gaps between buildings that the bunnies were now traveling parallel to him. He continued to skate to the next cross street, then swerved left—directly into the path of the colony of bunnies.

"YAYAYAYAYAYA!" yaya'd Mr. Taffle, as he dodged around the bunnies. This caused many of them to bounce nastily into each other and spill their bags of bunny marbles on the street. The spilled marbles caused the rest of them to crash into a massive bunny pile. It would have been slapstick perfection if not for all the screams of agony and horrifying broken bones protruding out of the bloody bunny costumes. Mr. Taffle disappeared down the alleyway on the other side of the street, skating in and out of back routes like a possessed maniac. He glanced behind him. He seemed to have lost everyone. But then he turned back just in time to catch the Farmer Ted 8s' Winnebago about to plow into him. By now he knew this wasn't just by chance. The pants were screaming out to all the freaks to "come and get some." Mr. Taffle flew off the skateboard moments before the Winnebago ran it over, which rocketed the skateboard right back at him, clipping his legs and sending him slamming to the ground.

Once again he found himself surrounded by the Farmer Ted 8s (all covered in the insides of a cow) with Farmer Ted 5 (the only one drenched from head to toe in frothy milk) pointing his harpoon gun down at him, ready to shoot.

"No way! Not going to happen! I'm the frog king! I can do anything!" howled Mr. Taffle in an uncanny impression of a stumbling-drunk Jim Morrison.

"Sword Guy sure does know how to make a speech."

"He could have pulled all the babes at the Toastmaster socials."

"Before or after he's harpooned?"

"Is that another trick question?"

Mr. Taffle stood up dramatically, as if this was somehow a superpower.

"I'm wearing the Pants of Insanity, and you have no power over me, so there!"

"Who should tell Sword Guy he's brainless?"

"Without a brain."

"A duh-duh-duh-duh-duh dummy."

"Who is gonna get a harpoon in the…"

"…tum-tum-tum-tum-tum stomach."

Mr. Taffle stumbled back in an attempt to get away. Shockingly, the Famer Ted 8s all stopped in their tracks, promptly turned around, and walked away.

Mr. Taffle was just as baffled as he was relieved. He couldn't stop himself from asking, "Where are you guys going?"

"We can't harpoon you if you're not inside the borders of Very, Very, Very, Very, Very Funkytown."

"They're not our stupid rules and regulations."

"They're the Duchess's stupid rules and regulations."

"You're not lying."

"I'm not lying," sighed a relieved Farmer Ted 5. "I've got to tell Barb!"

CHAPTER TWENTY-ONE
The Taffle Tells

I bet Mr. Manley's vulture capitalism neon sign would have looked really neat in claymation, thought Mr. Taffle, as he raced towards it.

He finally made it to the front of Mr. Manley's "The Treehouse." It was a luxury loft that was indeed shaped like a four-story-tall Blue Chinese Wisteria tree. He desperately hit the bark buzzer on the bark front door.

"Who this?" yawned Mr. Manley through the intercom.

"It's Mr. Taffle!"

"If you want to come up, you're going to have to use your phone to transfer over to me a hot new crypto currency called Demented Tickling Coin."

"My phone got ruined when I jet-packed into a canal. But I'm good for it! I swear!"

Then there was silence for a good 15 seconds.

"Hey, are you still there?" finally asked Mr. Taffle.

"Of course, I just thought you were maybe going to try to say something clever or stupid. Okey dokey, you rascal. Come up for a second diet soda of my second computer's choosing."

The door opened, revealing it to be the door to an elevator.

The inside of the elevator was a shrine to the Macho Manley Mustache and Man Perm Hall of Fame. "Tom Selleck, of course... Lionel Richie, duh... Oates from Hall and Oates, okay... But who in the hell is Lee Horsley?"

The elevator door opened on the fourth floor, where Mr. Taffle was greeted by Mr. Manley wearing pajamas from the TV series *Matt Houston* (played by Lee Horsley) while holding a can of soda in one hand and his pinwheel in the other.

"Here's your second diet soda," said Mr. Manley He handed Mr. Taffle a diet celery soda. For no apparent reason, Mr. Taffle crushed the can against his head, spilling it everywhere.

"Woah, looks like someone is going to have a serious case of the cocktail flu tomorrow," said Mr. Manley, followed by four slow winks.

"I'm not drunk from drinking booze. Jack Honey Badger shot some of his Honey Venom Badger Sauce into my eyes."

"Mr. Taffle, your orientation into the Loosey Goosey has transformed you into one seriously sick puppy—and it's really, really working for you," Mr. Manley proudly concluded.

"I HAVE A STRONG SUSPICION THE GHOST OF ALEX TREBEK AND HIS MIME MINIONS ARE GOING TO HURT THE MANNEQUIN MADAM... AND I NEED YOU TO HELP ME STOP THEM!"

"Say no more," said Mr. Manley as he blew into his pinwheel. "Let me just go slip on some shin guards, and we're out the door."

"I need to get these cursed pants off first!"

"Duh, of course you do."

Mr. Taffle removed his shoes and socks. "I'm also going to need to borrow... some underpants... as well as some shoes," he said, as he walked past Mr. Manley.

"I don't have any extra underwear I can spare, but you're more than welcome to borrow an adult diaper, as long as you promise to return it. Oh, I also see you're missing your baby toes," remarked Mr. Manley, as he snapped his pinwheel in half and gave it to Mr. Taffle. "Follow me."

They entered his Ancient Roman Bathhouse, with its fine mosaic floor, marble-covered walls, and replica statues of all the most famous Greek sculptures. However, each of the sculptures bore Mr. Manley's face. Mr. Manley chucked Mr. Taffle a wadded-up adult diaper he had stored inside the left leg of his pajamas.

"I'll be right back with some alternative pants for you, as well as some 99-Cent-Store flip flops," Mr. Manley said as he walked out of the room.

Mr. Taffle glared down at his pants. "Good riddance, pants. Not going to miss you AT ALL." (He wished he could have thought of a clever burn, but nothing came.) Mr. Taffle attempted to unzip the fly, but it wouldn't budge. He used his other hand to help. After a long struggle, he finally got the zipper down a quarter of the way. Then he had to take a break to catch his breath. The pants clearly didn't want to be taken off. This process was repeated six more times before the pants were finally unzipped. But even then, the pants still clung to his skin for dear life. After another lengthy battle with the pants, interspersed with several long breathers, he was finally able to peel himself free. He was left with bright red rashes and splotches of ripped-off leg hair, but he felt victorious.

But as Mr. Taffle slipped on the adult diaper, he could swear he heard the pants giggling at him. This straight-up pissed him off more than anything ever had. This was obviously his "FINAL JEOPARDY!" and Mr. Taffle vowed to himself, "I WON'T BACK DOWN, LIKE TOM PETTY, YO!" He bum-rushed the pants and slammed them down to the ground a dozen times. This was followed by a mad-dog flurry of uppercuts to the crotch. He put the pants into a headlock, while continuously kneeing the pants with blistering force. Again, he had to take a minute to catch his breath before continuing. Finally, he lasso-whipped the pants above his head 17 times before chucking them brutally hard against the ceiling.

As the pants bounced off, Mr. Taffle attempted to punt kick them... but he missed, Charlie Brown style, causing him to stumble wildly across the room. To break his fall, he grabbed onto the breasts of Aphrodite of Knidos. Again, this was yet another amazing coincidence: not only was this the only female Greek statue in the bathhouse, but he had stumbled upon the only way to access Mr. Manley's secret room.

The wall of the bathhouse opened like a clunky garage door, revealing an electronic ticker tape running across the back wall that read: "Welcome to Mr. Manley's War Room and Fun Center." Beneath the ticker tape was an electrical color-coded chart that read: "RED - ARCH ENEMIES, BLUE - SCUMBAGS, GREEN - AMOEBAS, YELLOW - NON-THREATS, ORANGE - ALLIES."

There was only one name, messily written in red ink, under Arch Enemies: "Taffle, Mr."

"Arch enemies?" he asked himself in disbelief. He opened the filing cabinet under the Arch Enemies label. The entire cabinet was dedicated to "Taffle, Mr." He skimmed through folders labeled "Intelligence, Coordination, Desires, and Bench Press."

"Holy crapola!" His right eyebrow flew into Spock position, followed by a pinch of his left nipple, as he yanked an encyclopedia-sized folder out of the file cabinet. It was titled: "THE TAFFLE TELLS."

"HOLY CRAPOLA!" he once again screamed, as he spotted the six television monitors on the wall. Each monitor had a marble nameplate underneath it: "Mr. Taffle's Living Room"; "Mr. Taffle's Bedroom"; "Mr. Taffle's Bathroom"; "Mr. Taffle's Volvo"; "Mr. Taffle's Mother's Bedroom."

"Holy crapola," he stated—calmly this time—as he noticed four mimes glaring at him diabolically from the opposite side of the room. He instinctively knew the only way out of this would require him to psychologically outsmart them by digging deep into his past. Mr. Taffle pretended as if his left leg had just cramped up. He grabbed hold of it, appearing to be in excruciating pain. But as soon as he fell to the ground, he rolled right back up and bolted for the door. This was the infamous "Taffle Trick-Out" he had previously mastered to avoid getting beat up in high school whenever he ventured out of his social bubble. But the mimes had already been briefed on the Taffle Trick-Out, so they didn't fall for it. Instead, they encircled him and expertly *mimed* him into an imaginary box. This caused Mr. Taffle's brain to overload, and he promptly passed out.

"And now, please, give a big round of applause for the host of *Jeopardy*... ALEX TREBEK!" a game show announcer's voice exclaimed from hidden speakers. Mr. Taffle awoke with a start. He slowly opened his eyes to the machine gun-like flashes of paparazzi cameras. He didn't notice the four mimes behind him. They were posed for the pictures as if they were walking a dog, pulling a rope, being sucked into a tornado, and leaning on an imaginary table.

"Oh, if one of those isn't going to become my new magnet pic hanging center stage on my deprivation tank," gushed Mr. Manley, camera in hand.

"You do always say the answer before I ask the question, and I've always thought that was so rude!" shouted Mr. Taffle. "He's never on your mind, but you're always on his. Well, I certainly get that clue now."

BAAAAAAAAA! A loud game show buzzer blared.

"You are incorrect," stated Mr. Manley, as he removed his macho manly wig to reveal a tattoo of Mr. Taffle's face covering his entire bald head. "I think the best way to explain this tattoo of your face on my bald head would be in the form of one of your precious fun facts," he said. "Now, in the wild, seeing the eyes of the tiger signifies that, well, you're about to become tiger chow. Because right before a tiger attacks, it turns its ears forward so the spots on the back of each ear faces nearer to its prey. The eyespots on the back of the tiger's ears serve to confuse predators and reduce the risk of attack from behind. Hence, once someone sees these eyes, the tiger is about to attack."

"That's actually a pretty interesting fun fact. But you've wasted your time with me. You were right all along. I do totally suck."

BAAAAAAAAA! The game show buzzer once again interrupted.

"You are incorrect again, Mr. Taffle! You see, for the last four, and soon to be, five years in a row, I've remained the Mighty Warlord because I made sure I find, and then take out, and I DON'T MEAN FOR DINNER, A MOVIE AND THEN MAYBE DANCING... that special perky upstart with that look in his eye. A look that says I'm a tenacious machine that will stop at nothing until I'm the Mighty Warlord."

"Well, I honestly thought you became my mentor 'cause you felt sorry for me, so I guess that's not all bad," he said, sounding more than a little bit proud of this fact. "But it still doesn't add up. I mean, you sent me to Mr. Ziska's house to try to save the deal."

"You're right, that doesn't add up. But it doesn't have to if Mr. Ziska had just received a death threat an hour before you were set to show up unannounced. Honestly, I'm glad you never went there and got arrested. I worked so damn hard hiring a think-tank to come up with the original plan to bring your ex-dream girl back so she could seduce you and you would ditch the Mighty Warlord Ceremony and run away with her for a—"

"PERMANENT VACATION TO LOVELY YUMA, ARIZONA!" continued the Game Show Announcer.

"Stop lying. She would never go along with this!" Mr. Taffle shouted back with no confidence.

The mimes covered their eyes while pretending to swallow an egg still in the shell.

"Sorry, Mr. Taffle, but that kooky broad loves only two things... money and that mannequin," he said with a bite that seemed destined for a viral meme.

"I think we've both learned something important today. You've learned just how crucial it is to be detail-oriented when crushing anything in your path on the way to five consecutive Mighty Warlords, even if it means tattooing your nemesis's irresistibly punchable face on your head to represent that they're always on your mind, and then to endure the constant throbbing of pain across your head and hands from constantly smacking it. Now, what I learned is that when your number-one team looks you dead in the eye and mimes to you that they can become expert mimes...YOU BETTER LISTEN TO THEM!"

The mimes then mimed like one of them had just recovered an onside kick, while the other four viciously blocked for him, and then scored a touchdown at the last second to win the Superbowl.

"Well, I once again have to skedaddle. I'll be sure to say *what up* to Mr. Winkie's surprised guest model as she crowns me the Mighty Warlord. Peeps are going to lose their minds when they find out Ms. Herpes Simplex is in the house!"

The mimes *mimed* like they were bobbleheads during an 8.6 magnitude earthquake as the wall dramatically closed behind them.

Mr. Taffle felt like crap in every way possible. And being curled up in a fetal position dressed in an adult diaper certainly didn't help matters. And the fact that he could now hear the pants giggling at him didn't help at all. Then, out of the blue, the third wall opened back up. It was Monique standing upright, dressed in a long, asymmetrical, 18k-gold formal gown, holding a note in her hand. Mr. Taffle rose to his feet, pulled up his adult diaper, and read the note:

"Meet me in sauna room number 7. It's the only room that isn't bugged."

Mr. Taffle, carrying Monique under his arm, opened the sauna door. The steam billowed out, dramatically revealing The Mannequin Madam standing in the center of the sauna, dressed in the same gown as Monique.

"Sorry I didn't dress up," sarcastically chimed Mr. Taffle.

"That's okay. I'm only in this fancy shmancy gown because I'm presenting the award for the Mighty Warlord. It's part of the deal I cut with Mr. Manley."

"So, it's really true," he said, as *the brutal pain machine with rechargeable batteries* once again returned.

"Stan, I made a huge mistake. Mr. Manley offered me so much money and prizes, and I thought it might be fun to get back into acting. So, I just—"

"Well, I think you're a great actress."

"Thank you."

"You're welcome." .

"I knew the second I laid eyes on you at The Truth what a massive mistake I had made. You have the kindest eyes I've ever seen, Stan, and that includes Baby Yoda. That's why I know love at first sight is a real thing. But I was so scared he was somehow listening, 'cause he's always listening. You've got to believe that I wanted to tell you what was really going on. That's why I went off-script into an improvisational flurry and came up with those additional riddles."

"Well, I guess you really do excel at improv after all," he said this time with a cartoonish level of sarcasm.

"Yes, I was totally surprised at how well I did with it," she said. "Look, I got completely lost in Very, Very, Very, Very, Very Funkytown. I didn't even realize how much my personal seesaw had become unbalanced. And when you're unbalanced, things can become confusing. I've made some terrible choices."

"Ya think?"

"Yes, I do think so. Stan, you know, I don't carry around a now-decapitated duplicate mannequin because I fancy myself some avant garde artist. I carry around a mannequin because it makes me feel normal. I'm just not the perfect dream girl you think I am. I'm screwed up, and I screwed up. But I want to make it right."

"There is no such thing as a life discount."

"What?"

But instead of answering, Mr. Taffle turned around to leave.

"Where are you going?" called The Mannequin Madam.

"I'm going to return the pants, and then I'm going home. I just want to go home."

Chapter Twenty-Two

One Final Squeeze

As Mr. Taffle walked into the Keytar Clothing and Pipe Shop, Le Rat casually glanced up from the final page of his erotic Napoleon novel. Even though he saw Mr. Taffle carrying the leather pants under his arm while still wearing only his adult diaper, Le Rat looked as if he couldn't care less about seeing Mr. Taffle again.

"You managed to get out of the Dinner Party," said Mr. Taffle with a relieved smile.

"And you managed to come to that conclusion all by yourself. Now, if you'll excuse me, I'm about to find out if Napoleon gets one final squeeze before he's exiled to the island of Saint Helena."

Mr. Taffle gently set the pants down on the counter in front of Le Rat. "Enjoy your book and have a nice life," he said. He took one final look at the pants and then turned around. A half a second later, the pants smacked him straight in the back of his head, as Le Rat masterfully chucked them at Mr. Taffle.

"Does this look like a thrift store to you?"

"Look, you were right about me and these pants, okay? I can't be trusted to be responsible for them. Because whatever I do, I will screw it up because I suck. So, just take them back, please," said Mr. Taffle. He picked up the pants and tossed them back to Le Rat.

"The pants are yours, Taffle," Le Rat casually replied as he threw them back, again, tagging him in the head.

"Not anymore," Mr. Taffle replied. He threw them back once again, only to have them again whipped right back at him, this time hard in the face. They repeated this back-and-forth nine times in a row, Le Rat nailing him perfectly each time.

On the ninth throw back Le Rat finally screamed, "YOU ARE NOT GLOWING ANYMORE!"

"Wait! Don't I have to be wearing the pants to glow?"

"I don't make the rules! She does."

"Who is 'she'?"

"She is the lead cow prankster I was telling you about. She comes to me in my dreams every night with riddles, all the while performing gymnastics and practical jokes. The riddle she gave me last night was in the form of a crossword puzzle. In it, the combination of six down and 13 across informed me that THE PANTS ARE YOURS! NOW, GO!"

Mr. Taffle took this in, processing what this crossword puzzle answer could mean.

"Okay. But before I go, I need for you to finish telling me why you never warned me about the pants in the first place."

"You swear if I tell you that you will leave?"

"I swear."

"Great news!" celebrated Le Rat with multiple fist pumps. "Okay, the night after I received the shipment of the Pants of Insanity, the lead prankster cow, who insists that she's my best friend, gave me the answer to an unknown question. I saw her sitting on the top of a 30-cow pyramid, and then she somersaulted off and into a split. This caused both of her swollen udders to burst open like milk balloons. It was nauseating. She explained to me that I would need to figure out what this question was before I would be allowed to warn anyone glowing about the insanity of the pants. And if I didn't listen to her, then the spirit of my favorite sommelier Catfish would be turned into cottage cheese."

"It was in a question/answer, like in *Jeopardy*?"

"I don't watch reality shows, Taffle," scoffed Le Rat.

"What was this question/answer?"

"PISS, PISS, PISS! I JUST TOLD YOU THAT I CANNOT TELL YOU!"

"BUT I'M NOT GLOWING ANYMORE, RIGHT!"

"GOOD POINT, TAFFLE!" Le Rat took a deep breath. "When this animal is placed in boiling water, it will jump right out. However, if it is placed in cold water that is slowly heated, it will not perceive the danger and will be cooked to death.

"What is the frog?" confidently answered Mr. Taffle.

Le Rat was astonished that Mr. Taffle knew the answer. "Well, I'm still not sure of the significance of this riddle."

"The boiling frog story is generally told in a metaphorical context with the upshot being that people should make themselves aware of gradual change lest they suffer eventual, undesirable consequences," stated Mr. Taffle. This was a fun fact he had memorized correctly.

"Well, that makes sense. I mean, how does that make sense?" frantically asked Le Rat as his nostrils spastically rotated. Oh, how Mr. Taffle loathed this nostril rotation. Or used to loathe it. He didn't care anymore.

"I'm the frog," winked Mr. Taffle playfully as he scooped the pants off the floor, then swung around his back and through his legs, as skilled as a Harlem Globetrotter, before heading out the door.

Mr. Taffle strutted down the street like a man who definitely knew how to strut now. In fact, one passerby said, "Yo, Baby Travolta, put on a shirt!" And even though he was still wearing an adult diaper, he could feel a strong *sizzle* percolating between all eight of his toes, as well as the two stubs where his baby toes used to be. Without breaking stride, he slipped the pants back on perfectly and then... *WHOOOOOOOOOOOOOOOOSH!* The electricity engulfed his entire body.

WHAT THE HELL IS THAT?! he thought, as he passed a sexy stewardess the very moment her double scoop cookies n' cream ice cream cone started falling from her hand. Mr. Taffle snagged the ice cream out of the air, took a monster lick, and then handed it back to her.

"Thank you, Mr. Badass," she said to him matter-of-factly.

HOLY CRAPOLA! At that moment he realized that he was now riding on top of a *SIZZLING* BLUE WHALE!

The crowded sidewalk parted for him as they felt this almighty *sizzle* coming through. It communicated loud and clear that Mr. Taffle did indeed own these or any streets blessed enough to have him strut down them. His strut turned into a jog, then into a run, and finally into a sprint.

Chapter Twenty-Three

The Fifth Annual Mr. Winkie's Mighty Warlord Extravaganza

I t was standing room only in The Mighty Chief Den, and the dead silence of anticipation that fell over all the salesman screamed what a big deal this day was. It also showed just how great a job the Top Doggies had done brainwashing this belief system deep into the employees' psyches. Over a 30 second period, one could hear each of the 106 employees whisper, "This is, like, so spiritual."

The Mighty Chief Den was located underneath the Mr. Winkie Corporate offices, and its steel vault door was opened only once a year for the big ceremony. The same "Shock and Awe" advance metric that Money Ball Analytics had used to create the rest of the building's design had also made this ceremonial den a sacred place.

In addition, the computer had determined that the Mighty Chief Den should be modeled after the two levels of the Fort Knox main vault. This included 1500 usable gold toilet chairs in the center of the vault that wrapped around a rotating gold American Eagle coin stage. The Big Gong sat on top of a 20-foot former K-pop band's pyramid. This had been acquired at a steep discount when the band broke up mid-tour. Also included in the deal was the part of the K-pop lighting rig that could cruise around the stage remotely and blast strobe lights and lasers directly over the Big Gong (as well as in the corneas of anyone in the crowd that wasn't paying attention). A diamondoid spike, which proudly held up the Mighty Warlord crown, stood off to the left of the Big Gong. The Mighty Warlord crown was an amalgamation of pieces from several cultures that had been appropriated distastefully. There was a little bit of a Native American headdress, a tad of a Zulu hat, a dash of a Samoan tuiga, and a crumbling of a Chinese Tassel Gold Phoenix crown, not to mention all the fake cucumbers randomly sticking out. One-hundred-ninety-five flatscreen televisions representing every country in Mr. Winkie Electronic Global Army and Family's international domain were lowered from the ceiling on motorized mounts. This was all under the watchful glare of the 50 taxidermized bald eagles that hung on wires to simulate that they were flying above while randomly pooping out silver dollars. Each flat screen was in the shape of the country it represented. There were some difficulties with the feed coming from the Maldives, and nobody actually showed up to the Andorra meeting, so technically there were only 193 countries participating.

"WHO'S READY TO *SIZZLE!*" roared The Branch Manager (dressed in the same classy equestrian pantsuit of the USA Olympic team) through her cordless headset microphone as she fist-pumped her way onstage.

"FO SHIZZLE, MY NIZZLE?!" hollered back the entire Mr. Winkie Electronic Global Army and Family. They continued to chant this call and respond as if their lives depended on it.

"THE MEAT STARTS TO *SIZZLE*!"

"THE JUICE GETS LOOSE!"

"WHAT YOU GOING TO DO?!"

"LAP IT UP!"

"WHAT ELSE YOU GOING TO DO?!

"SLURP IT IN AND SUCK IT DOWN!"

"*SIZZLE! SIZZLE! SIZZLE, SIZZLE! SIZZLE! SIZZLE, SIZZLE!*"

"And now, Mr. Winkie sales soldiers from around the world, for the first time ever, a very special Projecto will be projectoed to us directly from an undisclosed island fortress. You may know him as the head honcho, the big cheese, boss man number one, or the other Son of God, but I know him as the genius who just gave me a sweet raise! Please, give a major blast of *sizzles* to MR. WINKIE'S PROJECTION!

Deafening *sizzles* echoed around the vault as the 92-times-bigger-than-normal projection of Mr. Winkie shot out of every salesperson's Projecto headband and appeared above a series of flame ball torches and reddish pink smoke machines shooting up from the stage. This was an obvious homage to the Wizard of Oz. That is, it was to everyone but Mr. Winkie. He had always taken pride in the fact that he would never admit to ripping anyone off, no matter how obvious the theft. The only difference was that Mr. Winkie's projection was being filtered through a periwinkle purple. This color was chosen as it was determined to be the most effective color to disguise the constant sweat that poured down Mr. Winkie's forehead. But the "Echo" effect on Mr. Winkie's voice had had to be changed to a "Phaser" effect; the legal department worried about a potential blowback from the Oz Estate.

"WELCOME TO THE FIFTH ANNUAL MR. WINKIE'S MIGHTY WARLORD EXTRAVAGANZA!" roared Mr. Winkie as river of sweat gushed down his face (revealing that the periwinkle couldn't cover it up after all). "Wow, it feels like just yesterday that I successfully bid on that abandoned storage unit that yielded the ultra-rare Wade Boggs Commemorative Coin Set that allowed me to self-fund Mr. Winkie's first product, the Dissolving Sweet and Low Burner Phone, 'Make an untraceable call, and then sweeten your coffee.' Who would have guessed that would be such a worldwide smash hit? Except for me, of course. And as I see representatives of the Mr. Winkie Electronic Global Army and Family from all around the world, I'm so humbled that—despite the vast differences of our cultures, race, and the tolerance for torturing our own citizens—I'm so proud of what an amazing company I've created. Okay, I was going to say some more stuff, but I don't feel like it. So I'm not going to, as I can do whatever I want. And that's the power every one of you should be striving for! Now, what I really want to do is to introduce to you to this year's Mighty Warlord supermodel presenter. So, misses and misters, I present to you the lovely and super pretty KATRINA VAN BUREN!"

A secret ramp lifted out of the floor on the far end of the vault. Theatrical fog with beams of light shot out, spectacularly revealing The Mannequin Madam, still carrying Monique. It looked like a big-time pro wrestling entrance. As she made her way to the stage, it was clear from the look on her face that she would rather be literally anywhere else in the world. The Mr. Winkie Electronic Global Army and Family went wild with applause, as well as a barrage of catcalls.

"ISN'T THAT MS. HERPES SIMPLEX?!"

"WHY IS SHE CARRYING A MANNEQUIN?!"

"SHE'S SO HOT!"

"I'M NOT INTO MANNEQUINS ANYMORE!"

"WAIT, WHAT?!"

The Mannequin Madam read straight off an index card with zero emotion. "Good evening, Mr. Winkie Electronic Global Army and Family. Well, it's been a wild year growing our Projecto sales force in order to infect the real and virtual worlds. And so, this year, we're going to make everyone a Mighty Warlord. Start to laugh like you mean it, and then say I'm just kidding. So, let's find out who is going to be this year's Biggest Champ, aka The Mighty Warlord." She pulled an envelope out from inside Monique's gown and opened it, but she didn't even bother to fake-read it. "This year's Mighty Warlord is Mr. Manley."

Mr. Manley made sure he was sitting on the farthest possible gold toilet from the stage so he could milk the ceremonial riding of the invisible elephant on roller skates, which he had already started doing before The Mannequin Madam had even finished announcing his name. The announcement set off the entire sales force in a soccer hooligan-type mania. As Mr. Manley galloped through the aisles of toilets, all the employees made a mad dash towards him in hopes of being one of the lucky ones who would receive a *sizzle* heat check. A few dozen people were trampled, but that was expected and already accounted for in the lawsuit budget. "I felt Mr. Manley's *sizzle*, and now the bones in my hand actually feel like they're melting away!" celebrated a lucky employee from the IT department, as she withered in ecstatic agony.

Mr. Manley dismounted from the air elephant and jumped on the stage. The Mannequin Madam was there to greet him with the Mighty Warlord crown. He tried to kiss her, but she quickly blocked it with the back of Monique's neck stub.

"I don't know why you're being such a party pooper. You're going to totally dig your free weekend in Laughlin, and that includes a one-hour free rental of an electric lounge-chair boat," sexily whispered Mr. Manley. He then put on the Mighty Warlord crown, dropped to his knees, looked up, and lifted his arms in praise. "Before I bang the Big Gong and make this official, I want to give a big thanks to the big guy upstairs... Zeus the OGG. I know all the strings you pulled to make this happen, you little smoothie, and I want you to know I really appreciate all of your time and tricks. And I'd also like to thank..." Mr. Manley stopped mid-sentence as he realized that all the employees had their backs turned to him and were instead looking at...Mr. Taffle?!"

Mr. Taffle stood on top of Mr. Manley's abandoned toilet, still shirtless and shoeless, and with the The Taffle Tells folder under his arm. He was master *sizzling* while activating the Loosey Goosey technique at its highest level. "WHOA!" Everyone in the vault could feel it (except for Mr. Winkie, since he was just there as a projection).

"Who is this *clinky, clanking, clattering collection of caligulous junk that has dared to disturb the great and powerful* Mr. Winkie's Mighty Warlord Ceremony?" he bellowed, impersonating, and plagiarizing the *Wizard of Oz*, which was again obvious to everyone but him.

"Mr. Manley has been conspiring against me and against the entire company!" announced Mr. Taffle. "I've got the Mr. Taffle file right here. You'll find a load of ATTENTION TO DETAIL evidence that proves he's been spying on me and many of you... and that includes you, too, Mr. Winkie! In addition, he's been sabotaging other people's deals for the last four years, including the record-setting deal I made with Monetary Financial. They didn't cancel that deal; Mr. Manley did!"

The Mannequin Madam stepped forward. "IT'S ALL TRUE! I WAS HIRED BY MR. MANLEY TO BE ONE OF HIS MONKEYS... IN HIS BARREL OF MONKEYS!"

Ear-splitting gasps erupted from the crowd, as well as from 193 of the 195 other countries.

"What the hell is going on, Mr. Manley?" asked a confused Mr. Winkie, totally dropping the Oz camp.

"Okay, I'll go ahead and let the boy out of the bubble, but first, I want to announce that I'm going to have to resign from my position as Mr. Taffle's mentor, and having that blemish on my once-perfect resume stings a little bit. Secondly, I really wanted everyone to get a chance to celebrate me one last time before I leaked to the press my mammoth announcement. But just like I said in Paragraph 17 of the Loosey Goosey Report, when another opportunity presents itself, you don't have to be choosy; all you got to do is unleash the Loosey Goosey. And I wasn't even trying to rhyme! So, here's the scoop... and I'm just going to use the strong verb, short sentence technique for the greatest impact possible. By CAPTURING my fifth Mighty Warlord, I'm RAKING in the miscalculated stock options and CASHING them in, and then CREATING Mr. Manley's Electronics, where I'll be LAUNCHING those two Mr. Winkie apps, by legally STEALING them and then LAUGHING hard. Oh, yes, THAT app," he said with a pelvic thrust. And with four more thrusts, he continued, "And, oh yeah, uh huh, uh huh, THAT OTHER ONE!"

The projection of Mr. Winkie was in deep concentration as to what his next move should be. Or at least he was trying to appear like he was deeply concentrating; he was using the now-familiar Spock eyebrow tilt technique.

Finally... "Okay, I might just have a solution to this. Mr. Manley. Ummmmm... you're fired."

Mr. Manley coolly took off his wig, revealing his Mr. Taffle tattoo. "I'm the guy who will tattoo you on my head if I don't like you, so take what I'm about to tell you with the utmost seriousness.

I'm offering every employee around the world, including Canada I guess, a 10% bump in your salary. And I will QUADRUUUUUUPLE your current stock option. This is a ONE-TIME ONLY OFFER. ANYONE WHO WANTS IN ON THE PIG-OUT, STAND NOW WITH ME, MY BROTHERS AND SISTERS!"

At first, only one of the salespeople stood up. But then another... and another. This was happening in all the other countries as well. Before long, over half of every conference room around the world was standing.

"You dare try to pull a fast one on the great and powerful Mr. Winkie, you *billowing bale of bovine fodder*," roared Mr. Winkie (right back into his *Wizard* routine). You're not this year's Mighty Warlord, so you don't get that bonus. I'm evoking section 7.6 of Tablet 3 of the Mr. Winkie Charter, which states that I can do whatever I want if I feel threatened."

"Section 19.2 of Tablet 12: Once you are named the Mighty Warlord, you are the Mighty Warlord, no erases."

"Section 1 Table 1, Clause 5.4: It's not official until the Mighty Warlord bangs the Big Gong!"

There were four seconds of complete silence before Mr. Manley made a beeline for the pyramid that held the Big Gong, in order to bang it.

"DON'T LET HIM BANG THE BIG GONG!" screamed Mr. Winkie.

This was the final spark that ignited the CHAOS OF ALL CHAOS. It was now an all-out rumble, pitting every employee of the Mr. Winkie Electronic Global Army and Family around the world against each other. Here are some of the highlights of the total mayhem: Ms. Potter from Accounting wrapped her Projecto around Mr. Calabro, the President of the International Legal Department's neck; a nameless intern gave a gold toilet swirly to the Director of

Special Events; and the head of Custodial Services kicked over his dirty mop water bucket and rolled around in it like a dog on a hot summer day.

Mr. Manley expertly ascended the extremely steep pyramid. After all, he had already done it four times previously. There was no way it was going to be humanly possible for Mr. Taffle to make it through the bedlam in time to stop Mr. Manley from banging the Big Gong. That is, until the pants took over for him, and he magically sped up, leaping from one gold toilet to the next as if he were still the claymation frog hopping across lily pads in hyperspeed.

Mr. Taffle hopped onto the stage, hopped all the way up to the top of the pyramid, and then hopped on top of Mr. Manley's shoulders. They tumbled right off the pyramid. Mr. Manley ended up directly on top of Mr. Taffle, pinning him to the ground.

"Sorry, Mr. Taffle, but it turns out I still got the most *sizzle*, and you don't, so na nanny na nah," he teased. He prepared to strike with the gong mallet.

At that very moment, the Mannequin Madam suddenly swung Monique the Mannequin like a golf club, square into Mr. Manley's face. She knocked him out cold. He plunged off the stage, landing on top of the Chief Business Development Officer, who was squatting on the IT manager's head. And, in a matter of seconds, all the fighting both in the vault and around the world ceased.

"Thank you," said Mr. Taffle to The Mannequin Madam.

"You're welcome," she said to him.

"May I use your microphone?"

"Sure."

"Thank you."

"You're welcome."

Mr. Taffle stood up, picked up the gong mallet, and addressed the astonished crowd.

"Last night I approached a 60-foot tall Bloody Mary goblet filled with mermaids sliding down a celery stalk into a tomato pond filled with horseradish sea horses. Some of them rode around the goblet on pickle-spear sea scooters chucking beach ball-sized olives at each other. And I specifically remember thinking, *This is the most ridiculous thing I've ever seen.* But what was even more ridiculous was that it might not have even been in the top 10 of the most ridiculous things I had already witnessed that hour. However, nothing I experienced last night felt as ridiculous as this moment, when I'm about to bang that Big Gong."

Mr. Taffle dropped the gong mallet. The entire room hushed in disbelief. After a few moments, The Mannequin Madam whispered in Mr. Taffle's ear. "I totally get what you mean... but I have to admit I think it would be kind of hot to see you bang the Big Gong."

"I'M GOING TO BANG IT ANYWAY!" declared Mr. Taffle. He picked the mallet back up. He lit the head of the gong mallet off one of the shooting stage fireballs and then slid on one of the Projectos around his head. The crowd burst into applause.

Mr. Taffle hopped all the way back up to the top of the pyramid. And as the loudest collective *sizzle* in the history of *sizzling* ricocheted throughout the vault, Mr. Taffle raised the flaming gong mallet over his head like a fierce Fun-sized Norse Warrior. He turned his head and eyes toward the Big Gong. He made sure his chin was touching his front shoulder, that his grip on the mallet was tension-free, his upper body was relaxed, and that his hands were positioned close to his back shoulder.

He war cried, "AHHHHHHHHHHHHHHHHHHHHHHHHHHHHH-HHHHHHHHHHHHHHHHHHHHHHHHHHHHHHHHHHHHHHH-HHHHHHHHHHHHHHHHHHHHHHHHHHHHHHHHHHHHHHH-HHHHHHHHHHHHHHHHHHHHHHHHHHHHHHHHHHHHHHHH-HHHHHHHHHHHHHHHHHHHHHH!" He then swung the mallet with irresistible force. He hit the gong so fiercely it plummeted off the pyramid, nailing the Chief New Media Officer in the stomach.

Suddenly, the entire vault shook a little. The 195 conference rooms of all the other countries trembled as well. In a matter of seconds, the shake turned into an 8.6-magnitude earthquake. Everyone ran for their lives as the taxidermied bald eagles rained down from above and the gold toilets exploded into water fountains of liquid gold.

"Oh, my God, it's the Feel technology," realized Mr. Taffle. "My *sizzle* was too powerful!" He immediately shot a concerned look down the pyramid, making sure The Mannequin Madam was okay. She was more than okay. She was smiling like someone who was truly happy for the first time in her life.

"STAN, I ALWAYS KNEW YOU WOULD ROCK THE WORLD!" she called up to him.

"THANK YOU!"

"YOU'RE WELCOME!"

THE END.

Hey you've finished the book! Take a deep breath, that bizarre twitch in your left eye will go away soon... hopefully... no promises. But this is just the beginning! You can get exclusive access, insights, deals, discounts and dad jokes for all things Daniel Eric Finkel at danielericfinkel.com/SignUp.

Also, if you want to scramble your brain some more, please give the Mr. Taffle's Pants of Insanity soundtrack a listen on all streaming platforms including Spotify at: https://open.spotify.com/artist/3CiVCGUsRn6hjzcRIpFKEL?si=9Z-5DkYAQc2RTLjHV_h3BQ

Daniel Eric Finkel lives in Highland Park, CA where he likes to take hikes with the ghosts of his deceased dogs. He's written countless screenplays and sometimes writes raps about them. Like this one...

About the Author

I'm Daniel Eric Finkel
Not Ray Goddamn Finkel
Laces out ain't this jingle
Not trying to make a single
This is for my book
That I wrote
It's a clever way for me to
promote
And gloat
About my book
Cause it's a hit
And my spit is legit
So I came up with this shtick,
So you would read it
and share it
on your social media pages
I know what the game is!!!!!!!
To be creatively courageous is outrageously contagious
And I may just,
stain my name on your melted brain with lyrical flames about the
pants that are insane.
INSAAAAAAAAAAANE!

ACKNOWLEDGEMENTS

As I'm starting to write this, I'm realizing there's just way too many people to acknowledge and I would definitely forget some key people that deserve praise for helping and collaborating with me on my creative life long adventure. I have much love and appreciation for all of you.

I decided I would thank the six people that made it through the first draft of the book. I now know what a HUGE accomplishment that was. The other people that at least tried, I thank you from the bottom of my heart... but I still can't put you in the acknowledgements. You blew it.

Now don't freak out my awesome family! Like my Uncle Bob Rubin, the legendary sports journalist and author, I will also dedicate all of my future books to family members. My sister and I got a dedication to the book *Big Men of the NBA*. You'll get your *sizzle!*

So THANK YOU:

1. Joey Capone
2. Jerry Curl
3. Monica Khudan
4. Esther Miller
5. Jeremy Nance
6. Tommy Taretta

Oh wait! I'd like to give a big thank you to the memory of Sarah Geller. She made a fanzine for the band The Serotonins (I was lucky enough to be in so shout out to all of them) called The Taffler many years ago. Yes, the history of this project could have its own book. Sarah was so giving, creative and had a huge heart.

I'm remembering that I promised my super cool foster sister and hall of fame dentist Geri Okamoto that I would acknowledge her in the book after she saved my mouth for like the 174th time.

And now I better give a big hug to my real sister Patricia Finkel for giving me some great final notes. She's the best!

Also, this legend Ryan Johnson (who I've barely spoken to in years) sent me a donation out of the blue just because he wanted to support my art. What a legend! Of course, I promised I would acknowledge him in the book.

I'd also be such a jerk if I didn't give major props to the two genius musicians who joined forces with me to write and produce a soundtrack for the book: Jerry Curl and Marcus Junkin. And let's give a shout out to the incredible Justin Phelps at The Hallowed Halls recording studio in Portland. And another one to the mastering guru Ian Sefchick.

Oh damn! I can't forget my amazing book cover artist Patricia Moffett. Or my equally amazing copy editor Ramona Soto. Or my legendary website designer Jesse "Y2" Shannon. Or "Uncle" Jesse Branhum from Third Eye Visuals for the dope author pictures.

Oh double damn! Do you see what's happening here? I'm doing exactly what I didn't want to do. Screw it. Let's also give some major shout outs to The 500 podcast with Josh Adam Meyers, Bradley Dujmovic, Rhett Dunlap, Paul Madonna, Watkins Story Lab, Dale L. Roberts, Dave Warden, Nate Tuck, Constantine Paraskevopoulos, Tyler Jenich, Emilia Richeson, The Larue family, Burgathon, Camp

Goofball, The Warlords of Rock n Roll Thunder & Lightning, and Flea from the RHCP.

And now it's guaranteed that I forgot a key person. I'm sorry and THANK YOU!

Made in the USA
Las Vegas, NV
18 December 2022

63388712R00128